For my niece and nephews—
Chessa, Steve, Dylan, and Jesse—with love

Rae slid off the sheet covering her canvas—and felt like all the blood had been drained from her body.

Her mother's face . . . Rae forced herself to really look at it. Acid, she decided. Acid had been splashed all over the painting, eating ragged holes in her mother's face. And then the canvas had been slashed with a knife.

Rae backed away until she hit the sink behind her. She leaned against it, her legs feeling too weak to support her. She looked at the painting again, and from this distance she realized that the slashes weren't random. They formed words—*Stop asking questions.*

Rae turned around, fumbled with the cold-water knob, and managed to turn it on, then she leaned forward and let the stream of water run over her face.

"Okay," she muttered as she straightened up. "So someone doesn't want me to ask questions." She pulled a couple of rough brown paper towels out of the dispenser and scrubbed her face hard, her hands shaking. Whoever it was, they had been here again . . . in her school. In her *art* room. They had touched her painting, ruined it. But they were scared, too, she realized. They didn't want her to ask questions because she was getting close to the truth—finally.

Don't miss any of the books in this
thrilling new series:
fingerprints

fingerprints

4

secrets

melinda metz

AVON BOOKS
An Imprint of HarperCollinsPublishers

Secrets

Printed in the United States of America.

For information address
HarperCollins Children's Books, a division of
HarperCollins Publishers, 1350 Avenue of the Americas,
New York, NY 10019.

 Produced by 17th Street Productions,
an Alloy Online, Inc. company
33 West 17th Street, New York, NY 10011

Library of Congress Catalog Card Number: 00-193287
ISBN 0-06-447281-7

First Avon edition, 2001

AVON TRADEMARK REG. U.S. PAT. OFF.
AND IN OTHER COUNTRIES,
MARCA REGISTRADA, HECHO EN U.S.A.

Visit us on the World Wide Web!
www.harperteen.com

secrets

Chapter 1

Rae Voight has finally discovered the truth about her mother. Every horrible detail. That knowledge is like a sweet taste in my mouth, a sweet taste dripping juice down my chin. If only I could kill her right now, right this second—

But someone else has been watching my Rae. And if I kill her now, the way I'm burning to do, I may never find out who it is. That could be dangerous—dangerous for me. This person wants Rae dead. But Rae and I are connected, in one of the deepest ways possible. And if that connection has something to do with why this other person is after Rae, then I could be the next target.

I don't think they know the truth about me. But I need to learn everything about them to be sure I stay safe. Without Rae my chance to gather information is lost.

So she has to stay alive. For now. But I won't be able to hold out much longer.

* * *

"Excuse me," Yana Savari called to the girl arranging sleeveless cable-knit turtlenecks on a table. "Do you have these in a six?" She shook the pleather pants she was holding in the girl's direction.

"I'll check the back," the girl answered, and headed off at a pace slow enough to show that she was doing it because she wanted to, not because she had to.

Yana shook her head. "She clearly thinks her poop could be made into designer jewelry."

Rae laughed. Yana could always make her laugh. Even when Rae had been in the hospital and Yana was a volunteer there, Rae had always ended up laughing at least once every time they talked.

"I know you love ordering around the help, but I don't wear size six," Rae told Yana.

"They have to be tight. That's the whole point," Yana answered. She narrowed her blue eyes. "Don't be trying to weasel out of our deal. I get to make you try on whatever outfit I pick—that includes size."

"When I agreed to this makeover game of yours, I didn't know that I'd be risking organ damage," Rae complained. She scanned the boutique, looking for the perfect outfit to put Yana in when it was Rae's turn to be makeover queen. It had to be something Yana'd hate. That meant cute and sweet and ultra-girlie. Maybe one of those—

A girl passed in front of the rack of skirts Rae'd been eyeing, and Rae quickly turned around and headed as far away from the girl as she could, ending up in front of the discount rack tucked in the corner of the boutique.

Not someone I need to run into, Rae thought, thumbing through the shirts on sale. If she had to, she could make chitchat with Jackie Kane, but it wasn't something she wanted to do. Not something Jackie probably wanted to do, either. They'd hardly spoken to each other this semester, and Jackie'd only shown up at the hospital for one visit, one group visit. Yeah, it was better for both of them if Rae pretended that she hadn't seen Jackie. Who knew—at this very moment Jackie could very well be pretending that she hadn't seen Rae.

"You're not actually trying to hide from me, are you?" Yana asked as she stepped up beside Rae.

"Well, you are pretty terrifying today. But no," Rae answered.

"Come on. I got the pants." Yana led the way to the dressing rooms and shoved Rae into the closest one with the clothes Yana'd picked out.

Rae unbuttoned her pale yellow silk shirt and slid

it off, then pulled on the Boys Lie T-shirt Yana'd chosen for her. It hit her just above the belly button. *Jackie wouldn't be caught dead in this,* Rae thought. She went more for the classy-sexy, where it wasn't totally clear that you were going for sexy at all. At least it wasn't unless you shopped with Jackie and saw how totally calculating she was. She felt a little pang thinking about shopping with Jackie. It was like she was thinking about another girl—a girl named Rae who looked like Rae but who was an alternate-universe Rae.

Yana's lots more fun, anyway, Rae thought. She stripped off her khakis and started working on the pleather pants. She had to lean against the dressing-room wall and stretch her legs out in front of her to get them zipped.

"Let's see you." Yana rapped on the flimsy rattan door of the dressing room.

"One sec," Rae called back. She straightened up, inspected herself in the mirror, and frowned. She pulled the Boys Lie T-shirt a little farther down to cover the top of her belly button because she didn't like the weird little dimply thing in the center, then stepped out of the dressing room.

"It's the antiyou. Exactly what I was going for," Yana said. She dragged Rae over to the long mirror at the end of the row of dressing rooms. "Yep. The complete opposite of your prep school khakis and little sweater sets. Or it would be if you hadn't left on the bra. That T-shirt should come with a label—hand wash, cool iron, no bra." Yana reached over and fluffed Rae's curly reddish brown hair, studied her for a moment, and gave a satisfied nod.

"Just don't tell me to go pantyless," Rae answered. "I think you could do serious damage to yourself wearing pleather with no protection."

"Oh, yeah. That's your real problem with—" Yana stopped abruptly. "You've got to see this," Yana whispered, leaning close to Rae. "The Barbie who just came out of the dressing room is walking away with about five hundred dollars of merch. That stuff she has on the hangers—those are the clothes she wore in here."

Rae looked in the mirror and caught sight of Jackie pushing her way through the daisy-patterned curtain that separated the dressing rooms from the rest of the store.

Jackie. The girl whose nickname with the guys was Snowball because she could be so chilly. The girl who knew exactly where she wanted to go to college, what job she wanted, how many kids she was going to have. Getting nabbed for shoplifting couldn't be part of her famous life plan.

"I know her. She goes to my school," Rae told Yana, realizing she hadn't responded.

"I'm not surprised. It's always the rich wenches who shoplift," Yana said, a vein of bitterness running through her voice.

Rae didn't want to get into a conversation about rich people versus poor people with Yana. The fact that Rae and her dad had so much more money—mostly from an inheritance of Rae's mother—than Yana and her father did always felt icky. She wasn't going to go anywhere near there.

"I used to be friends with her," Rae added. "Like eat-lunch-every-day, hang-out-most-weekends friends before, you know, I did my impersonation of a crazy person in the caf at the finale of my sophomore year."

Yana hit Rae on the back of the head. She had this rule against Rae even getting close to calling herself crazy.

"Anyway, Jackie was never into anything like that," Rae continued.

"Guess she got bored with—" Yana shrugged. "Whatever it is you guys use to make your college applications look impressive. Reading to the blind or whatever."

"Maybe I should catch up to her and . . ." Rae let the words trail off. Like Jackie would take advice from the school loon.

"Yeah, go get her," Yana urged. "She probably didn't realize she left wearing the wrong clothes."

"Okay, dumb idea," Rae answered, even though there was this little part of her that felt like she should do *something,* that she shouldn't let a former friend, even a former friend who was probably repulsed by Rae, do something so stupid. She shook her head, trying to flick the thought away.

"Let me change. Then it's my turn to create the antiyou." She turned to face Yana. "Definitely going to need something that will cover the tats," she added, her eyes going to the DNA tattoo that circled Yana's belly button.

"If you're not going to get that T-shirt—which you should—I want it," Yana said. "I've been saving up for something new. Everything I own makes me want to puke," Yana called after Rae as Rae started back toward her dressing room.

"Walking around with the words *Boys Lie* blazing across your breasts probably isn't going to improve your social life," Rae warned over her shoulder. "And I'm getting you a guy by prom time—no matter what it takes." Rae pulled open the dressing-room door. It gave a squeak that sent a tingle from her finger bones all the way up to her shoulder.

"Wait. Rae, come back here. But try to look casual about it," Yana instructed, her voice intense. Rae turned around and saw that Yana's blue eyes were wide and her lips were pressed together into a thin line. Suddenly Rae could feel the air between them crackle with a current stronger than electricity. Fear.

Rae started toward Yana, heading back to the spot where the row of dressing rooms dead-ended at the long mirror. Her heart accelerated with every step, and it felt like the narrow corridor was closing in on her. She tried to act like a normal girl doing the normal shopping thing. "What's up?" she asked, her voice coming out too loud.

"We're being watched," Yana whispered.

Rae's throat closed up. She twisted the hem of the T-shirt with both hands, stretching out the material. "Where? Who?" she got out.

I am such an idiot, she thought. *God, like a store in the Atlanta Underground mall is some kind of safe place. Like whoever's been following me would be unable to cross the threshold of a boutique.*

"Slowly, look up and to the right," Yana instructed. "Past the edge of the mirror, right in the corner."

Rae obeyed, surprised she still had complete control over her body when her brain was sizzling with panic.

"You see it?" Yana asked.

Rae searched the wall, fighting the urge not to look, to just grab Yana's hand and run as fast and far as she could. But she didn't see anything out of place. Just the . . .

"You mean the security camera?" Rae asked, shoving the words through her tight throat.

"Yeah." Yana grinned, the tension slipping off her features. "I guess I meant we *should* be being watched," she explained. "Somebody's going to get their butt fired. They should have been all over your girlfriend."

A bark of laughter escaped from deep inside Rae. Then another one. She sank down onto the floor, laughter jerking out of her, so sharp edged, it brought tears to her eyes.

Yana sat down next to her and gripped Rae's shoulder tightly. "You okay?"

Rae couldn't answer for a minute. "Yeah," she finally managed to say. She let out another machine-gun burst of laughter. "But you should have heard what was going through my mind. I was thinking—I was thinking—" Laughter took her over again, cramping her stomach, making the inside of her throat feel raw.

Suddenly Yana winced. "Oh, Rae, I'm sorry," she said. "You were thinking what it's completely normal to be thinking. You were thinking I meant we were being watched by the psycho who tried to kill you." Yana gave Rae's shoulder a squeeze. "I shouldn't have joked around like that. Not with everything you've—"

"It's okay," Rae interrupted, all desire to laugh suddenly sucked out of her. "I don't want you to treat me like a—"

"Like a delicate prep school flower?" Yana cut in, using her fingers to comb her bleached blond hair away from her face.

"Exactly," Rae answered. "Now, let me change. Wait until you see the outfit I'm picking out for you. I'll get my revenge for your little joke. Don't you worry about it." She turned around and made her way back into the dressing room, the door giving its horrible squeak again as she closed it behind her.

"Oh God," she muttered, catching sight of her reflection in the dressing-room mirror. Her mascara was halfway down her cheeks. She licked her finger and started wiping it away.

What a total idiot I was, she thought. *Yeah, okay, some strange, weird, and very bad stuff has happened to me. But things are smoothing out a little. None of my friends has been kidnapped in weeks. It's been even longer since the attempt on my life. There hasn't been a pipe bomb waiting for me anywhere.*

Rae shook her head. What normal person was relieved just to say nobody had been trying to kill them lately? But still, her life *was* calming down. She hadn't even gotten one of those *gifts* from . . . whoever the hell it was that had sent her the box filled with cremated remains.

Rae forced a smile at her reflection, then licked her finger again—and froze.

Don't do this. Don't you do this again, she told herself. *Don't have another freak-out over nothing. You should still be in the walnut farm if you do.*

She pulled in a long, shuddering breath. "Just check it out," she said out loud. "It's going to be nothing, but you have to look."

Slowly, jaws aching, she opened her mouth as far as she could and peered inside. There, there near the back of her tongue, was a spot of . . . Rae leaned closer to the mirror, her harsh, hot breaths immediately clouding it up. She wiped the mirror with her sleeve. "It's not nothing," she whispered. There was definitely a small spot of fungus growing on her tongue.

She flashed on her mother's medical records, the memory of reading them so clear, it was as if the words had materialized in front of her face. One of the nurses had made a notation about a fungus on her mother's tongue. It was one of the first signs of her deterioration, of the wasting disease that progressed so quickly, she was dead before the doctors had the slightest clue what was happening.

So that's it, Rae thought. She knew she should feel more surprised, but this had been her fear for so long. She didn't want to be like her mother in any way. But she was, she was so, so much like her. And now she was going to die in exactly the way her mother had.

How long did she have? Months? Weeks? If it went exactly the way it had with her mother, Rae might only have days.

She felt the hysterical laughter begin to build inside her again. *Whoever's trying to kill me might not even get the chance,* she thought wildly. *My own body might beat them to it.*

Anthony Fascinelli shut his bedroom door, locked it, checked that it was locked, then checked it again. He walked over to his closet and opened it slowly. A bunch of flannel shirts. A corduroy shirt. A for-losers-only suit his mother had bought him a couple of Christmases ago. Anthony slammed the closet shut. He glanced over at his dresser but didn't bother to open it. He knew what was inside. T-shirts, mostly brown or blue. A couple from concerts. Plus that Backstreet Boys one his little sister, Anna, had given him.

"Can definitely eliminate that, at least," he muttered. He opened the closet again and jerked the closest shirt off the hanger. He yanked off the sweatshirt he was wearing and managed to get on the shirt, although he buttoned it wrong—twice, then let out something between a grunt and a groan and stepped in front of the mirror above his dresser. He tried to look at himself like a stranger would, a stranger who went to Sanderson Prep.

Short. That was the first word that popped into his head. Well, he couldn't freakin' do anything about that. He forced himself to keep looking. Was the shirt okay? He tucked it in, pulled it out, tucked it in again. "How the hell should I know?" he exploded.

He tried to remember what the guys—the ones he'd seen when he'd picked up Rae—were wearing. But all he could picture were their cars. The SUVs, the Beemers, the—

Anthony ripped off the shirt. A button pinged across the floor and rolled under the bed.

Screw it. He couldn't believe he was actually trying on clothes and checking himself out in the mirror like a girl. No matter how he dressed, it would take about a second for anybody at the friggin' school to know he didn't belong there. Oh, man, why had he let Rae talk him into this?

I could call her up, he thought. *Ask her advice.* Anthony rolled his eyes. He could just imagine that conversation. *Rae, I just don't know what to wear to my first day of school. Do you think the tan T-shirt*

13

or the navy T-shirt? I just can't decide what I look better in.

But his feet headed toward the door, anyway, and a few seconds later he was standing in the kitchen, staring at the phone. His stepdad, Tom, had the game blaring in the living room, so nobody would hear him—if he decided to make the call.

Like there was any *if* about it since his finger was already punching in her number. He stopped after the fifth number, because Tom barged into the kitchen, heading straight for the fridge. Anthony hung up the phone and grabbed a bag of chips out of the closest cupboard. *Just go on back to the game,* he silently told Tom.

Tom shut the fridge door, a couple of beers under one arm and a hunk of cheese already halfway to his mouth. "Those are mine. I bought them for the game," he told Anthony. He plucked the chips out of Anthony's hand on his way to the door.

Fine. Just go, Anthony thought. He did not need to be making conversation with Tom today.

As if he sensed that Anthony wanted him gone, Tom turned back when he reached the doorway. "So you start at that fancy ass prep school tomorrow," he said.

"Yeah," Anthony answered. Not much else he could say.

"You better be friggin' brilliant on the football field, that's all I can say." Tom took a big bite of the cheese, leaving his teeth marks in the cheddar. "And you better not get injured. It's not like they want you for your brains—you do know that, right?"

"Yeah," Anthony said again. He'd get rid of Tom faster if he agreed with him. Besides, as much as he didn't want to think of Tom being right about anything, everything the jerk had said was true. Anthony wouldn't be surprised if he ended up having to stay in the equipment closet whenever there wasn't a game or a practice. Which wouldn't be so bad. At least then it wouldn't matter what he wore.

"Just didn't want you to go walking in there with any delusions in your head," Tom said. He popped one of his beers and wandered off.

"Thanks, buddy," Anthony muttered. "Good to know you care."

He waited until he heard Tom start shouting at the tube, then he grabbed the phone and dialed Rae's number. As soon as Rae got out a hello, he started talking. He had to, or he wouldn't be able to get the words out.

"So, um, Rae, I was wondering—you know I'm starting at Sanderson tomorrow—" He stopped, cringing. He sounded like a complete idiot. He decided to try again. "What kind of—" He cut himself off again, then let out a growl of frustration.

Rae didn't say anything.

"Are you there?" he asked.

"Yeah," she answered. That was it. Just *yeah*. And normally he couldn't get the girl to shut up.

"You know I'm starting at Sanderson tomorrow," he repeated.

"Uh-huh," Rae mumbled. "Right," she added, her voice getting a little stronger. "So are you nervous?"

"Well, I'm calling to ask you what I should wear," Anthony blurted out. "Does that tell you anything?"

Rae didn't laugh. Or tell him not to worry about it. There was just another silence. "Um, that tan T-shirt looks good on you," she finally said. "It's not really a big deal."

"Okay. Well . . . okay. See you tomorrow." Anthony hung up without waiting for a reply.

She's more freaked than I am, he realized. He slumped down in one of the kitchen chairs. *It's like it just actually hit her that I won't just be going to Sanderson, I'll be going to Sanderson* with *her.* She could hardly even stand to talk about it.

A little snort of laughter escaped from him. He'd actually been thinking that maybe when he and Rae were at the same school, things might end up being different between them, like in a guy-girl kind of way. Clearly not going to happen.

Anthony scrubbed his forehead with both hands. If Rae didn't want him at Sanderson Prep, nobody would.

Rae positioned her largest sketchbook over her knees and stared down at the blank sheet of paper. Sometimes she thought better when she drew instead of wrote, like her thoughts ended up coming from a different, deeper part of her brain. And she needed to think right now—as hard as she could. There wasn't room for anything else but figuring out the truth— what was happening to her.

She frowned as she remembered the way Anthony had sounded over the phone. She'd never heard him like that. Scared was nothing new after everything they'd been through together. But he was seriously rattled about coming to Sanderson. She felt bad that she hadn't been much help, but she needed all her energy to focus on this.

Okay, she thought, looking down at the sketch pad. *My only shot at beating this thing—at staying alive—is to find out everything I can about my mom. Maybe there's something about her that can tell me why she got sick, something that can tell me how to . . .*

"This is hopeless," she whispered. But she picked up a pencil, one with a nice, soft lead, and sat up a little straighter, leaning against the pillows she'd propped against her headboard.

Okay, I need places to get more information about Mom. Her pencil started moving before a thought was fully formed, and in seconds she had a rough sketch of Scott State Prison at the top of the pad.

There was definitely someone at the prison who knew something about her mother. Rae'd picked up a thought from a fingerprint while she was there. Someone had been looking at Rae and wondering if she was born while Rae's mother was in the group. But Rae didn't know which of the prisoners had left the fingerprint. The thought could have come from any of the men who'd touched the basketball during the game going on when Rae'd toured the exercise yard. She didn't even know one name.

Okay, next, she thought. She doodled a little, writing her name and her mother's name side by side, then impulsively drawing a mental hospital around them both. They hadn't been in the same hospital, but hey, a little artistic license was allowed. Rae could go back to the hospital, have another chat with her mother's doctor. He'd been nice. But Rae didn't have the feeling he knew any more than what he'd told her—and what she'd read in her mother's chart when he was out of his office.

There's Dad, Rae reminded herself. She did a little sketch of him pulling the sword Excalibur out of the rock. It was hard to think of her father without thinking about her dad's beloved King Arthur.

That was one of the problems with her dad as an information source—he tended to see her mother like a princess from one of the stories he taught in his medieval literature classes. He saw Rae's mother as all good, all loving. Even after what she'd done. Even after he knew Rae's mother had shot her best friend in the head at close range. He wasn't exactly a reliable witness.

The best place to get facts was from her mother herself. But Rae had touched everything in the box of her mom's things—several times and on every inch of their surfaces. She'd gotten every thought it was possible to get. They hadn't told her much about the mysterious New Agey group, which Rae thought could be very important. All she'd managed to get was the name of someone in the group—Amanda Reese.

Rae drew a face almost obscured by shadow. She'd managed to find the phone number of

Amanda Reese and even talked to her daughter, who was also named Amanda. All she'd found out from Amanda the daughter was that her mother had been murdered a year before. Dead end. No pun intended.

Rae ground the point of her pencil into the paper until she tore a little hole, then she quickly drew another face covered in shadow. *Whoever's been following me could have all the information I need,* she thought. *They knew I have a power. Who knows what other information they might have?*

But I have no clue who they are, so that's a dead end, too. She crossed out the second shadowed face, and her eyes moved back to the first one. She started to cross it off, too. Amanda Reese couldn't help her.

Rae hesitated with her pencil hovering over Amanda's face. One Amanda Reese was dead. But one was still alive. Could the daughter of the dead woman know anything that could help Rae?

"It's so gruesome," Rae mumbled, wincing at the thought of asking Amanda a bunch of questions about her dead mother.

Then she let her tongue slip to the roof of her mouth, feeling the rough patch there. She was calling the doctor first thing tomorrow morning. But there was a good chance the doctor wouldn't have a clue what was wrong. And someone else out there could have the information Rae needed.

Rae shivered. She didn't want to bring up raw feelings for Amanda Reese. But Amanda might be her best chance at finding out what she needed to know—Rae's best chance at saving her life.

Chapter 2

Rae shifted slightly. The thin paper under her butt tore a little, letting the cold metal of the examination table touch her bare thigh. How much longer was she going to have to wait in here? The nurse who'd weighed her and taken her temperature and blood pressure had said the doctor would be in in a few minutes. That had been at least twenty minutes ago. She shifted again. The paper tore again.

The fungus is getting bigger, Rae thought. She could almost feel it growing, almost taste its flavor with every swallow. She stuck her forefinger in her mouth, fighting her gag reflex, and tried to feel the fungus spot. She needed to know exactly how big it was now. As she started to trace it, there was a quick knock on the examination-room door. A second later Dr. Avery stepped into the room. "It's good to see you, Rae," she said.

Rae whipped her finger out of her mouth. "You too," she answered, trying to get over the weird feeling of talking to someone who was fully clothed while she was half naked.

Dr. Avery flipped open Rae's chart. *God, it's thick enough to be an eighty-year-old woman's,* Rae thought. Thanks to all the tests they ran on her after her meltdown.

"So you have a growth on your tongue," Dr. Avery said. "Let's have a look." She turned to the counter across from Rae and pulled a tongue depressor out of a glass jar, then moved up in front of Rae, so close, Rae's knees were almost touching the doctor's stomach. "You know the drill. Say ahhh."

Rae did, and a second later she felt the dry wood of the depressor against her tongue. She hated that sensation. It made her teeth feel static-filled.

Dr. Avery moved the tongue depressor slightly, leaning a little closer. Rae could feel the doctor's breath against her cheek and even smell the orange Tic-Tacs Dr. Avery had in her mouth. *What do you see?* Rae wanted to shout. It felt like the doctor had been staring into her mouth for an hour, even though Rae knew it was less than a minute. Probably less than fifteen seconds, really. She gripped the edge of the table—

/Is it cancer?/*shouldn't have*/

—so she wouldn't start squirming. The thoughts she picked up gave her a double dose of anxiety, the last thing she needed when she was already so freaked. She hadn't been able to wear wax on her fingers the way she usually did when she didn't want to get fingerprint thoughts, because she'd been afraid the doctor would notice and think it was strange. Strange was the last thing Rae wanted to be in front of any kind of doctor.

Dr. Avery took the tongue depressor out of Rae's mouth and tossed it in the white metal wastebasket. "I think what you've got is a mild case of strep throat," Dr. Avery told Rae. "It's not unusual for the tongue to be affected like this. I'll just do a culture to be sure." She prepared a swab and ran it across the back of Rae's throat.

"So, I, um, don't have some weird fungus or mold or anything?" Rae asked, struggling not to sound too worried. Rae liked Dr. Avery, but the doctor knew Rae's mental health history, and Rae didn't want to set off any warning bells.

Dr. Avery smiled. "Nothing so exotic." She did a quick check of Rae's ears and nostrils and massaged the glands on the sides of her neck. "Everything else looks fine."

A wave of relief washed through Rae, so strong, it made her dizzy. *Strep throat. I have strep throat.* It was like hearing she'd just won a trip around the world. Her mother definitely hadn't died from an extreme case of strep. This was totally, totally different.

"Anything else going on? Any questions while you've got me?" Dr. Avery asked. Rae noticed that she was going for the casual-voice thing, too. *Probably doesn't want me to think she's at all concerned about the possibility that I could lose it again someday.*

"No. I've been feeling good," Rae answered. Then she remembered the numb spots. She'd been so freaked out by finding the spot on her tongue that she'd forgotten about them.

Dr. Avery picked Rae's chart up off the counter. "Stop by my office when you're dressed. I'll give you a prescription for some antibiotics."

"Actually, there is one thing," Rae blurted out. "It's probably nothing, but sometimes I get these numb spots." She tightened her grip on the edge of the table, the metal pressing into her fingers.

"Numb spots," Dr. Avery repeated, her gaze sharpening on Rae's face. "Where?"

"Different places. The back of my neck once. The tip of my finger. Um, on my leg. A spot on my arm." Rae watched the doctor's face tighten slightly.

"How often does this happen?" Dr. Avery asked. She pulled a pen out of her pocket and flipped open Rae's chart.

"Just, I don't know, maybe five times," Rae answered, her body seeming to harden, as if in another few seconds she'd be incapable of moving.

Dr. Avery made a notation. "And how long does the numbness last?"

"The spots usually fade in less than a day," Rae told her, managing to get her mouth to open and close.

Dr. Avery nodded as she scribbled another notation. *Guess she's not going to tell me it's all part of the strep throat or some minor skin condition,* Rae thought.

"Have you made any changes in your diet?" Dr. Avery asked, her voice crisp. Rae gave her head a tiny shake.

"You haven't eaten any seeds or nuts that you don't usually eat?" Dr. Avery pressed.

"Uh-uh," Rae forced out.

"Well, I think we should definitely keep tabs on this," the doctor said. "What I want you to do is keep a written record of these periods of numbness—are they after exercise, when you wake up, after you eat, that kind of thing. Make another appointment in two weeks and bring in your notes. We'll go over them together."

"Okay," Rae mumbled.

"Go on and get dressed now." Dr. Avery glanced at her watch, then hurried out of the room. The second she closed the door behind her, Rae started to tremble. She wished there was a fingerprint she could touch to know what Dr. Avery really thought about the numb spots. Unfortunately, the doctor hadn't touched anything but Rae's chart after Rae told her about the numbness, and Dr. Avery had taken the chart with her.

Rae half jumped, half slid off the examination table and grabbed her pants, picking up a few of her old thoughts. As she dressed, she tried to remember exactly when the numbness spells had happened.

She'd gotten one that day in the pool when Anthony was teaching her to swim. And she'd gotten one the night Anthony had almost robbed that house with his new buddies. Oh, and one the day she and Yana had gone to see Big Al to get info about Anthony's father.

It always happened on days that I made fingertip-to-fingertip contact with someone. Not just on those days, but starting after she'd made the contact. The realization was like an explosion in Rae's mind.

So the numbness was connected to using her power. She'd considered that already, but it was becoming hard to avoid that it had to be the truth.

Was her mother's disease connected to using *her* psychic abilities? Rae felt like someone had just dropped an ice cube down the back of her shirt. Her trembling escalated to shivering. Even without the tongue thing, there was still too much similarity between her mother's life and Rae's.

Rae grabbed her purse and got up. This was pointless—she should never have even mentioned the numb spots to her doctor. What could Dr. Avery do, especially without knowing the reason they were happening? And it wasn't like Rae could tell her *that*. She'd just tell the doctor that the numbness had gone away, and skip that whole follow-up appointment thing.

She grabbed the knob.

I need to do some research on Rae's I

Dr. Avery touched the doorknob after I told her about the numb spots, Rae realized. And it worried her. Rae could feel the doctor's emotion swirling around in the fear already blasting through Rae.

I've got to find out the truth about my mother, Rae thought. *The entire truth. It's time. It's way past time.*

Anthony hesitated outside the cafeteria. Going into classes as the new guy was one thing. Hitting the caf, that was something else.

Yeah, because what if no one will let you sit with

them, he taunted himself. *What if somebody's mean to you? You big freakin' wuss.* He pushed open the double doors and headed to the food line. *Much better selection than at Fillmore,* he noted as he grabbed a foil-wrapped burger, a bag of chips, and two chocolate milks. After he handed over his cash, he turned toward the tables. He caught sight of a fro-yo machine out of the corner of his eye. Unbelievable.

He started a methodical table scan. Open seat at two o'clock, but a couple of the people at the table were actually playing chess. Pass. There were a bunch of open seats at the table dead center of the room. Suspiciously many. Pass.

Where does Rae sit? The thought managed to snake its way into Anthony's brain, pissing him off. He wasn't looking for Rae. He was looking for a place to park his butt.

"Fascinelli," someone yelled. Anthony turned his head toward the voice and saw Marcus Salkow waving him toward a table—a table that was clearly *the* table.

Anthony headed over and sat down in the empty seat across from Marcus and next to this blond girl who should be an ad for blond girls.

"You guys, this is Anthony," Marcus announced. "He's the new running back." Marcus nodded toward the blond girl. "That's Jackie." He pointed to the dark-haired girl next to him. "That's Lea. You know Sanders and McHugh from the team."

"Hey," Anthony muttered, wishing they would all stop looking at him and go back to whatever it was they'd been talking about.

"So where are you from?" Jackie asked. She popped one grape into her mouth, and Anthony had to force his eyes away from her lips. This girl was so out of his league.

"Uh, I just transferred from Fillmore," Anthony answered, talking to her forehead. This girl could be one of the Gap girls he fantasized about. Suddenly he realized he'd just said it out loud— admitted where he came from. He steeled himself for the obligatory awkward silence or uncomfortable reactions.

"Their loss," Marcus said without even a brief pause. "With Anthony on the team, we're gonna kick butt all the way to the state championships."

Anthony raised his eyebrows in surprise. Salkow was being decent. More than decent. There wasn't any reason for the guy to deal with Anthony off the field, but he was.

"Can I rub your head?" Jackie asked Anthony.

"Huh?" That's the only word his brain would come up with.

"It's this thing I do. I rub the heads of the football players for luck," Jackie answered.

"Since when?" the dark-haired girl—Lea—muttered.

Jackie ignored her. "So can I? I'm having this French quiz that I didn't study for after lunch, so I need some good luck."

"I'll give you some, Snowball," Sanders told her.

Jackie didn't appear amused. At least not until she looked back over at Anthony. Then her lips turned up and her eyes gleamed like she and Anthony were sharing a private joke.

She's flirting with me, Anthony realized, amazed. *This total Cardinal girl is flirting with me.* He wondered if everyone would know what the reason was if he casually moved his backpack into his lap. He decided not to risk it. He wasn't going to have to stand up for a while. He had time to get things back under control.

"Well?" Jackie asked.

"Sure. Why not?" Anthony lowered his head, and Jackie ran her fingers through his hair. The sensation of her fingernails against his scalp sent a blast of heat all the way to his toenails.

"You want to do my head, too?" McHugh called.

"No, Anthony left me supercharged," Jackie

answered, pulling her fingers through his hair a final time.

Was this actually his life? This couldn't possibly be his life. He was fat 'n' smelly Fascinelli, the guy who used to spend most of every school day out in the trailers where the "special needs" classes were held.

If this was real—if this was his life now, anything was possible. Even with—

Anthony tried to stop the thought, but it kept coming. Even with him and Rae. He could actually, like, ask her to go to the movies or something, something that didn't involve saving one of their butts. Maybe he could even—

Get a grip, Mr. Potatohead, Anthony interrupted himself. *Remember being on the phone with Rae yesterday? Come on, you can do it if you really try. Yeah, remember how she could hardly stand to say two words to you? Just stop right here and get a friggin' grip.*

But Anthony couldn't stop himself from checking the cafeteria for Rae, practically getting a crick in his neck from trying to see the tables behind him.

She wasn't there. *You're not the sharpest knife in the drawer,* Anthony told himself. *But even you can figure this out. She knows it's your first day. She's not in the cafeteria. Which means? Come on, you can do it.*

Rae couldn't care less that he was there. She obviously wasn't the least bit interested in hanging around him now that he was a part of her precious prep school.

Rae wandered around the house, trying to find something to do to . . . to basically keep herself from thinking about dying.

Maybe some sketching. She'd been thinking of doing some close-ups of her hand where she made the lines of her palm into a kind of drawing within a drawing. Something you'd have to look at twice to really see.

She headed into her bedroom and picked up her sketchbook off her desk. The two shadowy faces she'd drawn on her "list" stared up at her.

I shouldn't be drawing. I shouldn't be doing anything to distract myself. What I should be doing is going out there and finding out the facts I need. "I'm sorry, Amanda," she said, her voice coming out too loud in the silent house. "But I think that means I'm going to have to talk to you about your mom. I don't want to—"

Rae was jerked out of her thoughts by the sound of a car pulling into her driveway. Who was it? Her dad shouldn't be home for hours. Alice wasn't scheduled to clean. Who was it?

Adrenaline started pumping through her body. She felt like someone had stuck an IV of coffee into each arm. She rushed to the window. *Slow down,* she ordered herself. *Slow down. Fast moves draw attention.* She gently pulled the side of the curtain away from the window frame a quarter of an inch, then cautiously peeked outside. It wasn't a car out there. It was a truck. A guy in uniform climbed out and strode purposefully to the side gate. He disappeared into her backyard as if he had every right to be there.

Okay, no car out front. School day. He—whoever he is—has no reason to know I'm home. I'll just stay away from the windows and—

Uh-uh. No. She wasn't going to sit in the house like a scared little mouse. Rae ran to the back door and slammed outside. Maybe not the smartest move. But every muscle and nerve in her body were demanding action. She was going to find out exactly who was in her yard. And right now. "Where are you?" she demanded.

The guy in the uniform appeared from around the corner of the house. "Hey. I didn't realize anyone was home. I didn't mean to scare you," he said in a rush. He waved a clipboard at her. "Just here to read the meter. I'll be out of here before you know it."

"You didn't scare me," Rae told him, although she felt like her body had sprouted a heart at every pulse point. She could feel the little hearts pounding in her throat, her ears, her wrists, even her fingers.

Okay, meter reader, she thought. *Makes sense.* All her little hearts slowed down a little. Of course, how hard was it to get a uniform and a truck and say you're a meter reader? The hearts started speeding up again. *If you hadn't come out, who knows what the guy might be doing right now. He could be planting a bomb or—*

"Shouldn't you be in school?" the guy asked. He moved toward her, and Rae was hit by how alone they were. Most of the neighbors were at work. If the situation got ugly, no one would hear her even if she screamed her head off. And the closest phone was in the kitchen, which might as well be a thousand miles away. Definitely would have been smarter to be a little house mouse and just watch. Get information. Then decide what to do. But it was too late now.

The guy's green eyes narrowed, and Rae realized she hadn't answered his question. Well, why should she? He had no right to question her. And if she said anything right now, he might be able to hear how nervous she was.

"Guess it's none of my business," the guy said, his eyes darting around the backyard.

Looking for the meter, Rae realized. *He doesn't*

have a clue where it is. The little hairs at the back of her neck began to prickle. She swallowed hard. Then, willing her voice to stay steady, she asked, "Are you new?"

The guy took a step closer. *He knows I'm suspicious,* Rae thought. *Not good. Shouldn't have asked him if he was new. Should have acted like everything was normal.* Her adrenaline rush had faded. It had made her feel strong and powerful, like she could take on anyone. But God, the guy outweighed her by probably fifty pounds. And Rae was almost the worst person in her gym class. What was she doing out here? What had she been thinking?

"Nope. Been on this route for almost four years," the guy answered.

Yeah, right, Rae thought. *And in another year you'll be able to remember where the meter is.* She forced herself to nod and gave a little smile. If the guy figured out she wasn't buying his story, who knew what he could do.

Okay, so don't stand here until it's totally obvious to him that you know that he has no idea where the meter is. Back off. Let him think he's convinced you.

"I hear the microwave. My pizza's ready," Rae muttered, then headed back inside, trying to look like she'd completely lost interest in talking to the guy.

She returned to her bedroom and watched the truck. If she'd convinced him that she bought his story, he'd be gone in a few minutes. Her eyes began to sting, but she didn't blink. She wasn't looking away from the truck for even a second until she saw it drive away. Less than a minute later the guy came out and climbed in the truck and backed into the street. Rae watched until he drove out of sight.

Maybe he was really the meter guy, Rae thought. *Maybe he goes to so many houses, he just forgot where our meter is. Maybe I just created this huge drama out of nothing.*

Maybe that's what you want to believe. Maybe it's a little thing called denial. She sat down on her bed, picked up the phone, and dialed 411. Facts. From now on, it was all going to be about facts. She got the number of the power company, dialed it, and stayed on hold for about fifteen minutes. She asked her question and was put on hold again. A different man came on and told her that her house hadn't been scheduled for a meter reading that day.

"Thanks," Rae murmured. She hung up the phone, checked the clock, then snatched the phone back up again and punched in Anthony's number. He should have gotten home from school at least an hour ago.

The phone rang. And rang, and rang. "Come on,

Anthony," she whispered. He was the only one she wanted to talk to right now. No, not wanted to talk to, *needed.* The phone kept ringing. The answering machine didn't pick up. Reluctantly Rae put down the phone.

I'll try him again later, she thought. *And if I don't get him, I'll track him down at school tomorrow.*

Weird thought. It was hard to believe that Anthony was actually a Sanderson Prep guy. Weird, but good. She'd actually have a real friend at school.

Suddenly she got this flash of how it felt to have his arms around her that night when he'd told her what it was like to have a father who was a murderer. That night when she'd told him what she never told anyone—that her mother was a murderer, too.

When Anthony had held her that night, she'd felt like she'd been surrounded in a bubble of warmth, a place where nothing bad could ever happen. She'd never wanted him to let go.

So was she lying to herself? Was friendship all she wanted from Anthony Fascinelli?

Chapter 3

Rae headed toward the cafeteria Tuesday afternoon. Finally she'd get a chance to talk to Anthony. All this stuff was building up inside her. *Be honest,* she told herself. All this *fear.* About the non-meter reader. And about what was happening in her body. She'd never told Anthony the numbness she'd experienced that day in the pool wasn't a one-time thing. But as soon as she saw him, she would. He'd probably be pissed—Anthony hated it when she kept secrets, serious, possibly life-threatening secrets, from him. Rae didn't care. He could yell as much as he wanted. It would still feel so good to tell him everything.

As Rae headed past the girls' bathroom, her feet slowed down. She decided to duck inside, see if she needed any repairs. Last year this was her routine, hers and Lea's. They almost always hit the bathroom before the caf for hair and makeup touch-ups. Rae'd kind of gotten out of the habit, not that she walked around looking like a slob or anything.

She found a tiny section of free mirror space—no one nearby who'd expect her to talk to them—then pulled out a lipstick and gave herself a fresh coat, enjoying the smooth, moist glide across her lips. Next she added a little mascara and plucked a hair that had somehow sprouted between her eyebrows since that morning. Finally she sprayed a little no-frizz curl tamer on her hair and fluffed it. Did a quick overall inspection, checked her teeth for lipstick, then headed out, satisfied. More than satisfied.

Rae hurried to the caf with more eagerness than she'd felt in a long time. She pushed open the double doors—the layer of wax on her fingers keeping her from picking up any thoughts—and stepped inside. Her eyes immediately did an Anthony scan.

"Oh my God." The words popped out of her mouth without any conscious decision to say them. Anthony—Anthony freakin' Fascinelli—was sitting at her table. Well, her *old* table. He was saying something to Marcus that had Marcus cracking up. And Jackie—Jackie the *Snowball*—was running her fingers through Anthony's hair.

Rae backed toward the door, unable to take her eyes off Anthony. When she knocked into one of the long door handles, she turned around and stumbled into the hall, feeling dazed. *Definitely not the time to spill my guts to Anthony,* she thought. He wouldn't thank her for dragging him away from the group that pretty much everyone in school wanted to be in.

Or from Jackie's hands, she thought, wincing. She blinked, trying to clear her mind. Had she really just seen that? Anthony and Jackie? From the sick feeling in her stomach, she was pretty sure she had. Not that she cared, really. Except for the fact that she'd wanted so badly to tell someone what was going on with her. To tell Anthony.

So another lunch in the art room, she thought as she started down the hall. She shoved away the image of Anthony and Jackie, unwilling to focus on how much it hurt—or why.

The moment she reached the art room, she was glad she'd come. The smell of the oil paint had her fingers itching. She couldn't wait to get a brush in her hand.

Shirt first, Rae reminded herself. She'd ruined way too many clothes by getting so excited by her work that she dove right in without bothering to cover up. She snatched her long white shirt, actually an old one of her dad's, off its hook and hurriedly put it on, then set a fresh canvas on the easel she always used. Ms. O'Banyon wouldn't care. She'd given Rae permission to use any of the supplies she wanted.

Rae knew she should do some sketches first, think about composition. But she couldn't. She never could when she felt like this. She was entering the zone, the place where her hand had control of her body, not her brain.

Green, I need green, she thought. She selected a yellow-green oil and squeezed a blob on her palette, then added a glob of a green so dark, it was almost black. She caught up a brush small enough to give a clean line and thrust it into the dark green oil. She slashed a curve onto the canvas. Another curve. Another.

And out of those three curves came the suggestion of a face. Her mother's face.

Anthony locked eyes on the Lee High running back. *You aren't getting by me. Not in my first game as a Sabertooth. Try it and accept the pain.*

Marcus hiked the ball to Ellison. Anthony heard the ball smack into Ellison's hands. He knew in one second Ellison was going to spin and hand the ball off to McHugh. But that wasn't any of his business. His job was to be a human wall between the Lee running back and any of the key Sabertooth guys involved in the play.

The Lee running back feinted right with his hip. Anthony didn't buy it. He hurled himself to the guy's left. Their face guards hit with a teeth-jarring impact. And the guy went down—hard. It didn't look like he'd be getting up anytime soon, so Anthony took off for the goalpost. "I'm open," he yelled to McHugh, who'd collected a pack behind him.

McHugh twisted toward Anthony, and the ball came spiraling toward him. *You're mine, baby,* Anthony thought as the ball slammed into his hands. He tucked it under one arm, lowered his head, and pounded toward the goal. If he made it, the Sabertooths won the game. It was going to take a freakin' nuke to stop him.

He felt an arm loop around one calf. Not nearly enough, he thought. He pumped his legs like pistons, but the arm didn't release him. *You want to come? Fine,* Anthony thought. He plunged forward, pulling the guy along with him. He could hear people pounding up behind him, but the other guys on his team must have had the situation under control, because no one else touched Anthony.

A grunt jerked out of him with each stride. His legs were burning. The guy attached to him was getting heavier by the second. Didn't matter. All he could see now was the goal, like the white posts were standing at the end of a black tunnel. The sounds around him faded, his grunts going silent, the other players on the field, too.

His world narrowed down to the two white lines in the darkness. Almost through. Almost through.

Through. Color and sound exploded back into his world. "Fascinelli!" the crowd was shouting. He could hear the cheerleaders shrieking with joy.

Anthony spiked the brown ball into the brilliant green grass. Game over. Game won.

Suddenly his teammates were around him and he was in the air. When they put him down, it was in the locker-room shower—with his uniform still on. "Time for Anthony to bag the tiger," Marcus called out.

There was a cheer of approval from the other guys. Anthony scrambled out of the shower and shook the water out of his hair. He looked around for a towel. Before he could find one, the guys started yanking his clothes off. Anthony tried to fight them off, but in less than three seconds he was down to his jock.

What the hell was going on? Anthony stared around at the guys. They were all laughing and grinning. "Very funny," he muttered. He stalked over to his locker and opened it. Empty. Except for a ballerina costume.

"You'll get your clothes back when you've bagged the tiger," Marcus told him between snorts of laughter.

"What freakin' tiger?" Anthony demanded.

"The sabertooth in the assembly room," someone answered from behind him.

"Crap," Anthony said under his breath, picturing the big plaster Sanderson sabertooth on the assembly-room stage.

"Hey, we've all done it," McHugh said, slapping Anthony on the shoulder.

"In this?" Anthony used two fingers to pull the pink satin leotard out of the locker. The leotard had a friggin' *tutu* attached to it. All Anthony could do was look at it in horror.

"Yeah, in that," McHugh answered.

"It took us almost a month to get the tutu back from McHugh," Sanders related. "He thought he looked sooo pretty in it."

"It's either wear that or go home in your jock," Marcus said.

Anthony let out a low curse, then started to yank on the shiny leotard. It kept sticking to his skin, and it was too small, but he finally got it over his body.

"You just need one more thing," Ellison said. He pushed his way up to Anthony and carefully placed a rhinestone-studded tiara on his head.

"Make that two more things," Marcus said. Anthony backed away when he saw what Marcus held in his hand.

"No way," Anthony protested. But Marcus was already using the bright pink lipstick to paint Anthony's mouth.

"Okay. You're done. Now go get it and bring it back here," Marcus ordered.

Anthony squared his shoulders and headed out of the locker room—what else could he do?—trying to ignore the snickers from the guys and the knowledge that almost half his butt was hanging out of the leotard. To his relief the gym was empty. He trotted across the hardwood floor of the basketball court, his bare feet squeaking, then cracked opened the door leading to the hallway and took a peek. Empty. Anthony let out a breath he hadn't realized he'd been holding. *Okay, this is going to be no big deal,* he thought as he started down the hall, running this time instead of trotting, not pausing even when the leotard crept high enough to give him a massive wedgie. He wanted to be done with this little assignment and safely back in the locker room before anyone saw him.

He pushed his way through the caf's double doors and skidded to a stop, almost blinded by a dozen flashes of light. Camera flashes. Crap. Anthony blinked, and a cluster of smirking cheerleaders and pom-pom girls came into focus. A rush of heat flooded his face. He was freakin' blushing. Crap, crap, crap.

The longer you stand here, the more of a look they're all going to get, he told himself. He locked his eyes on the auditorium stage. It looked about ten miles away. *It's not going to get any closer if you don't start moving,* he thought. The only thing was, when he started moving, all the freakin' girls were going to get a good look at his butt cheeks. Not like the leotard exactly hid much up front. That realization got Anthony moving—to a chorus of catcalls from the girls. He wouldn't swear to it, but he was pretty sure that one of them pinched him, and he definitely felt a pom-pom shake its way down his back.

What felt like half an hour later—but was actually probably more like half a minute—he was up on the stage with the plaster Sabertooth balanced in his arms. At least the thing was big enough to keep all the critical front parts of himself covered. Now all he had to do was get himself back to the locker room. The only thing was, he'd have to go by the girls again. *Yeah, a bunch of scary, scary girls,* he thought.

"I. Have. Bagged. The. Tiger!" he yelled, then leaped from the stage and strutted toward the door. He was going to at least have a little dignity this time, no scurrying and blushing. The girls whooped their approval, and a grin broke across Anthony's face. He planted a big lipstick kiss on the cheerleader closest to the doors, earning himself a round of applause.

Anthony held the tiger over his head as he strode out of the cafeteria. As soon as the doors swung closed behind him, he bolted and didn't stop until he was safely back in the locker room. "You're a true Sabertooth now," Marcus called.

"So what do the girls do with those pictures they took?" Anthony asked, trying to sound casual.

"They'll be showing them to everyone at McHugh's party," Sanders told him.

Anthony nodded as if he knew all about the party. But he hadn't heard anything. Clearly he was good enough to be considered part of the team. Good enough to sit with the guys at lunch. But outside of school it seemed like it was a different story. Anthony was supposed to go back to his crappy little house and—

"You're coming, aren't you?" McHugh asked. "My parents are out of town for the week. It's going to be the most massive party of the year."

"Sure. Yeah," Anthony answered, feeling a ridiculously big smile trying to take over his face. "But I'm warning you guys, once the rest of the girls see those pictures, you're all going to be very lonely."

"Anthony's here," Rae's dad called up the stairs.

Rae froze, remembering the scene in the cafeteria at lunch today. Then she shook her head, telling herself she was being silly. She needed to talk to Anthony, and now she had the chance.

She got up and started walking toward her bedroom door, then stopped abruptly. She flipped her head down to her knees, then came back up fast so her hair went all full and curly around her face. *What are you doing?* she asked herself as she headed out of the room and down the hall. *It's just Anthony. He probably couldn't even say what color your hair is if he wasn't looking right at you.*

"Hey, did you see the game?" Anthony blurted out the second Rae stepped into the living room.

Rae blinked. "Obviously you didn't rush over here to see how I was feeling," she answered. She sat down in the chair across from him.

"What?" Anthony rubbed the bruise that was forming on his forehead.

"I was out sick," Rae said. "I thought you might have, you know, noticed." Actually she'd only been out sick yesterday. But she hadn't eaten in the caf today, so for all he knew, she could have been out two days running.

"Sorry," he muttered. "Are you okay?"

"I have strep," Rae told him. "But there's this—"

"It sucks that you missed the game," Anthony interrupted. "It was really close. I mean, it could have gone either way right up to the end, and I saw an opening and went for it. Pretty much won us the game."

"That's great," Rae answered, trying to force herself to sound enthusiastic. She wasn't the only one with a life here. This was a huge deal for Anthony. She could tell him all her garbage in a minute—about the numbness and the meter man who wasn't a meter man. But Anthony deserved to brag a little first. "I knew you'd be amazing," she told him.

"The guys actually carried me off the field," Anthony said. "Then they made me put on this ballet costume—"

"You bagged the tiger? After your first game?" Rae exclaimed. "Some guys aren't allowed to get near the tiger for a whole season. You must have blown the guys away."

"Nobody even cares that I used to go to Fillmore," Anthony rushed on.

"I knew they wouldn't," Rae answered. "So when I called you yesterday, you must have been at practice, huh? I should have figured."

"Everyone acts like I've always been around. They just assume I'll be hanging out with them," Anthony went on.

Thanks for asking why I called you, Rae thought, picking at a loose thread on the arm of her chair.

"This guy Marcus—Marcus Salkow, you know him?" Anthony didn't wait for an answer. "First day he calls me over to his table, introduces me, and man, this blond girl, Jackie, was—anyway. It's just like I've been going there since day one."

"I'm happy for you," Rae muttered, the image of Jackie's fingers running through Anthony's hair popping up in her mind. Not that it had been too far away ever since she'd seen the real thing . . .

She blinked a couple of times, as if that would get rid of the mental picture, which of course it didn't. It was like she had some kind of film loop running in her head.

You have a lot more important things to think about, she reminded herself. She opened her mouth to tell Anthony about the man she'd caught snooping around the backyard, but he was still babbling.

"All the cheerleaders took pictures of me with the tiger. Cheerleaders wanting pictures of me. How delusional does that sound?" Anthony asked.

Rae gave the loose thread a tug, making a snag in the upholstery. "Pretty friggin' delusional," she answered, her voice sounding harsh even to her own ears.

"Anyway, I wanted to tell you that one of the guys on the team—McHugh—invited me to a party tomorrow night. Parents on vacation. It's supposed to be huge. Probably there will be a ton of people you know there and I—"

"Considering I've gone to Sanderson since I was a freshman, yeah," Rae said, cutting him off. Clearly the only reason Anthony had come over was to tell her all about how great everything was. If she sat with him all night, he'd probably never get around to actually asking her a question. She had a lot to figure out. A lot of plans to make. If she had to do it without Anthony, fine.

"I might be going to the party," Anthony began again. "And I—"

He's never shutting up, Rae thought. "Look, you know what, my throat is kind of starting to hurt," she told him. "You should go. I don't want to contaminate you or anything."

Anthony slammed the car door shut. What in the hell had he been thinking? Was he insane? Did he think that he could just stop by Rae's and ask her to go to the party with him and that would be that?

The girl hadn't even let him get the question out. She kept interrupting him. Like she knew what he was going to ask and was trying to stop him from going there.

He let his head slump back against the seat. It wasn't just the idea that he was trying to ask her out that had gotten Rae all freaked out. She'd practically had icicles growing off her when he'd mentioned some of the people he was getting to know. Like she wanted nothing to do with any of it.

Did she even remember it was her friggin' idea for him to transfer? Hell, not even just her idea—she arranged the whole thing. Anthony straightened up and jammed the key in the ignition. He knew one thing for sure—he wasn't going to sit parked outside her house like the biggest loser in North America.

He turned over the engine, revving it until it growled, then he pulled out onto the street. About halfway down the block he spotted a car—if a BMW could be called something as basic as a *car*—pulling into Rae's driveway.

Anthony slowed to a crawl, eyes on the rearview mirror. The Beemer's door swung open—and Marcus Salkow stepped out. Anthony frowned, confused. He watched as Marcus slowly approached Rae's front door. Marcus was there to see *Rae?*

And the Bluebird finally gets it, Anthony thought, pressing his foot down on the gas. The old boyfriend Rae had at Sanderson—it was Marcus Salkow. Which more than explained why she wouldn't even let him ask her to the party. *When you're used to a guy in Salkow's league, you don't downgrade to a Fascinelli.*

Chapter 4

The doorbell rang about two minutes after Anthony left. Rae let out a groan. *Oh God, he's back. He forgot to tell me that one of the guys gave him the congratulatory butt pat after the game, something I absolutely need to know tonight.*

She stood up and headed to the front door, walking slowly. Maybe he'd take the hint and go away. The doorbell rang again. Typical Anthony. Rae picked up her pace and grabbed the doorknob, then jerked open the door. The coat of wax on her fingers protected her from picking up any thoughts. "Wh—" she started to demand. Then she realized it was Marcus standing on the porch.

He smiled at her, his trademark Salkow smile. It still kind of worked on her. Kind of. "Hey, I know I should have called first, but I thought if I called, you might tell me it wasn't a good time to come over, and then I wouldn't be here."

Rae snorted, then swung the door open wide. What choice did she have? "Well, since you're here, you might as well be here inside." Marcus headed for the living room as if he still came over almost every day, as if he hadn't ditched her and hooked up with Dori Hernandez while Rae was in the hospital. Yeah, he'd broken up with Dori. And yeah, he'd made it very clear he wanted Rae back. But still.

Marcus flopped down on the couch, legs apart in that guy way. "Make yourself at home," Rae muttered as she took a seat in the chair across from him.

"Great game today. Did you see it?" Marcus asked.

"No. I've been *sick*. Thanks for asking," Rae told him.

Marcus gave her the smile again. "You're cute when you're grouchy. Seriously, sorry you're sick. You want me to . . . get you something? Um, Kleenex?"

Rae shook her head. "I'm okay. The antibiotics have pretty much kicked in."

"It was fun at Sliders that time, wasn't it?" Marcus asked. He went into his Frankenstein voice, the voice he'd kept using when they'd had lunch at Sliders together. "Frrriennnd."

"Yeah. It was fun," Rae answered, her answer coming out sounding more tentative than she meant it to. And why wouldn't it? Her feelings about Marcus were all in a jumble. But that day at Sliders had been good. There had been actual moments when Rae felt like she and Marcus were Rae-and-Marcus again. She smiled at him, not a big Salkow kind of smile, but a smile. "Fuuunnnn," she added, doing Frankenstein herself.

"Okay, you admitted it was fun," Marcus said, leaning forward, his green eyes intense on her face. "And fun is good. People want to have as much fun as possible. Which means you're going to say yes when I ask you to go to the party at McHugh's with me tomorrow night."

Rae swallowed, hard. Yeah, he'd been acting friendly, trying to get her back. But this was a serious offer. An immediate one. She was glad she was sitting in the chair and not on the couch next to him. Even from this distance the Salkow magnetism was pulling on her. Anthony had some of that going, too. More than some. Maybe more than Marcus, even. When she was close to him, like in the car, she—

This is not about Anthony, Rae told herself sharply. *That big poo head.*

"You want me to run through that again?" Marcus asked. "I know it's sort of complicated. See, you admitted you had fun with me. People want to have as much fun as—"

"I got it the first time," Rae told him. Then she realized she should have let him keep going. It would have given her a few more minutes to think.

Did she want to go to the party with Marcus? It would make a statement, that's for sure. People would assume they were back together, even if they weren't. And Marcus, he'd make assumptions, too— that they were getting back together even if they weren't officially back together yet.

Rae felt thorny anxiety vines twining through her body. She wasn't ready for this decision. If Marcus was just asking her to eat lunch with him again, then it would be a pretty easy yes. But the party was a whole different deal.

I've got to say something, she thought. But she had no idea what it should be. Marcus seemed totally sincere. Still, just because he'd decided he wanted her back didn't mean that she wanted to be his girl-friend again. Even though she was pretty sure that's how he thought it worked.

"You know what, Marcus?" she asked. "I *am* feeling all right, but by the end of the day, I'm wiped. I can't see myself lasting through a party tomorrow night."

Okay, that should buy her a little time. She needed at least a little time to figure out what she wanted to do with Marcus.

"Oh." Marcus leaned back. "Well, you want to hang out for a while tonight? Watch some TV?" He stopped short. Rae knew he was remembering exactly the same thing she was. "Watch some TV" had been their code for making out when they were a couple because Rae's dad wouldn't allow a TV in the house.

"I actually meant TV TV," Marcus said. "I forgot—you want to play Monopoly or something?"

This is the equivalent of lunch, Rae thought. *Not public. Not something that will make Marcus think things have changed between us.*

But it was just too weird. The sofa was probably still warm from Anthony's butt. It would be kind of like he was still in the room with her and Marcus.

Marcus and Anthony. Anthony and Marcus. Her head started to hurt just thinking about the two of them.

"I'm pretty tired," Rae answered.

"Oh," Marcus said. "Oh." He stood up. "I should have called first."

Rae's throat tightened up. There was a time when Marcus showing up unexpectedly would have totally made her night. But things had changed. "Yeah, calling probably would have been better," she told him. She started to stand up.

"It's okay. Sit. You're tired," Marcus told her. "I know my way to the door."

The hurt in his voice almost made Rae want to call him back. Almost.

Anthony stood next to the directory in the main level of the Atlanta Underground mall. He had no friggin' idea what store he should go to. His mother had been so excited about Anthony going to his first Sanderson Prep party that she'd stuffed a wad of money in his hand and insisted he go buy himself "something nice to wear."

Which was cool of her. Showing up at the party looking normal—Sanderson Prep normal—would be good. Not that he cared that much. But what was normal? School normal? He couldn't even quite achieve that with the clothes he owned.

Anthony took a final look at the directory. Most of the store names meant nothing to him, so he jammed his hands in his pockets and started walking the mall, peering at window displays without getting too close. How could people actually shop for fun? When he reached the Gap, he decided to stop being a total wuss and go inside. It was the Gap. He could handle it. He stepped inside, pulling in a deep breath of that . . . clean, new smell all the stores in the mall had.

Okay. Now what? He headed toward a table with a pile of shirts on it. Girls' shirts. He veered away and started deeper into the store. A hand grabbed his elbow, gave it a light squeeze. Anthony jerked around and saw Jackie Kane smiling up at him. *Up* at him. That was nice. Rae was always eyeball to eyeball—unless she was wearing freakin' high heels. "Closet shopaholic?" Jackie asked.

"Yeah, right," Anthony muttered.

"Aw, it's okay. I'll be your mama. What are we shopping for?" Jackie answered, her blond hair gleaming under the store's lights.

Anthony swallowed hard, his mouth suddenly painfully dry. The way she said she'd be his mama—holy crap. It was like something out of one of his mental porn sessions. And Anthony was pretty sure that's what she'd been going for. Suddenly he realized he hadn't answered Jackie's question. "Clothes," he muttered.

"Goody. My fave," Jackie answered. She glanced over her shoulder. "Alicia, we have a job to do," she called to a girl Anthony thought was one of the pom-pom girls.

The girl hurried over. "What's up?"

"Anthony needs clothes—something for McHugh's

party," Jackie said, shooting Anthony a knowing smile. "And he, being a boy, needs help."

Alicia nodded. "First thing, we have to get you out of here. The Gap's fine for basics, but there's nothing here that really says party."

Jackie tightened her grip on his arm—she'd never let it go—and Alicia latched onto his other side. Together they pulled him out of the store. "I'm thinking Him," she said to Alicia.

"Good place to start," Alicia agreed. And they were off, towing Anthony between them. "But can we stop at Bangles for just one sec? I really need to drool over that bracelet a little more."

"Fine," Jackie said, rolling her eyes. "But not too long. Our agenda for the rest of the night is Anthony." They swung into a jewelry store that felt way too small to Anthony. Like one wrong step and he'd send one of the glass cases crashing to the floor.

The sales chick took one look at Alicia and pulled a silver bracelet from one of the cases. Alicia let go of Anthony and rushed over, making little crooning noises at the piece of metal. *She's like Anna with her cardboard tiara,* he thought, amused.

Jackie released him, too, and headed over to a display of earrings. Anthony wandered over and watched her try on a couple of pairs. *Rae would look good in those big hoopy ones*, he thought.

She'd need big ones to show through all that curly hair of hers.

He shook his head. Why was he thinking about Rae? She was the last person he should be thinking about right now. She'd made it pretty clear she'd be happier if he somehow disappeared from her world.

"One more minute, Alicia," Jackie warned, switching earrings again.

"No. If I look at it for one more minute, I'll buy it, and my parents will have a hissy if I put anything else on my Visa this month," Alicia answered.

"Tell you what," Jackie said. "I'll get it for you, and you can buy me something next month." She pulled her wallet out, then tossed an AmEx on the counter.

"Thanks, sweetie," Alicia cried, giving Jackie a smacking kiss on the cheek.

What planet have I landed on? Anthony wondered as he watched Jackie sign the credit slip. His mom had worked who knew how many hours for the money she'd given him tonight, and Jackie had just spent almost the same amount on a freakin' bracelet. And it wasn't even for her.

"Now it's all about Anthony," Alicia said when she had the little jewelry store bag looped over her wrist. She latched back onto him. Jackie grabbed the other side.

A few minutes later he was standing in Him—a store he'd never even heard of—with an armful of clothes. "Uh-uh. Stop right there," he told Alicia. "I am not even trying on those pants. They're silver."

She took a step closer. "They're hot."

"They're silver," Anthony repeated. "Forget it." These girls had clearly decided he was their own personal Ken doll, but they were wrong.

"How about these?" Jackie asked, holding up a pair of dark brown leather pants. Anthony actually thought they were somewhat cool, but he'd seen the price tag on another pair of leather pants, and he definitely couldn't go there.

"They make me itch," he told Jackie. "Look, I have too much to try on already. I'm hitting the dressing room." He bolted without waiting for Jackie or Alicia to answer. It's not like he needed their permission.

The first thing he did when he had one of the dressing-room doors closed safely behind him was a price tag check. That eliminated half of Jackie and Alicia's picks. He stared at the rust-colored suede—suede? Something like that—pants. They were in his price range, barely, but were they actually anything any guy would want to be seen in? They were actually more orange than rust. Who wore orange pants?

Anthony stripped off his jeans and started yanking

on the *orange* pants. He had them only half on when the dressing-room door started to open. "Someone's in here," he called. The door kept swinging open, and Jackie stuck her head in.

"I thought you might need help," she said.

"I know how to dress myself," Anthony told her, and firmly shut the door. He looked in the mirror, wanting to see what Jackie'd seen. Way too much, that was for sure. He got the pants up and zipped—and decided he looked like a dork.

He left the pants on, in case Jackie was still lurking, and grabbed the closest shirt. He didn't know what it was made of, but he liked the way it felt when he pulled it on. And the colors were good—different shades of brown. He checked the price tag. He could afford it—if he didn't get anything else. *If jeans aren't good enough for McHugh's party, screw it,* he thought. He got back into his own clothes as fast as he could, got the shirt back on the hanger, and headed out. "I'm getting this," he told Jackie and Alicia, who were hovering near the entrance to the dressing rooms.

"You have to model for us," Jackie insisted.

"No." Anthony went straight to the counter and paid with well-worn twenties. The guy behind the register looked at them as if he'd never seen actual paper money before. As soon as he got his change and his bag, he strode out of the store. Jackie and Alicia trailed after him.

"My boyfriend always gets cranky when he shops for clothes, too," Alicia said.

"I'm not cranky," Anthony protested. "I just—I need to get home."

"Me too," Alicia added. She turned to Jackie. "Thanks again for my bracelet."

"I got something for Anthony, too," Jackie announced, a little smile curling up one corner of her mouth.

"Whatever it is, take it back," Anthony said. "I don't need anyone buying things for me." Had she decided to take him on as a charity case or what?

Jackie gave him a playful poke on the chest with one finger. "Calm down. I didn't buy it." She slid a man's watch out from under the sleeve of her shirt and slipped it off her wrist.

"Jackie, God," Alicia exclaimed. "What if you'd gotten caught? Your parents—"

"I never get caught," Jackie interrupted. "Neither of you saw me get these, and you were standing practically right on top of me." She pushed her hair behind her ears to show off a pair of long earrings.

What was with the girl? That AmEx was only one of about a dozen credit cards in her wallet. It's not like she didn't have the funds for anything her little heart desired. Mommy and Daddy had made sure of that.

"I'm heading out. See you in school," Anthony said, pretending not to see Jackie's pout.

"What about the watch?" Jackie called after him as he headed for the closest exit.

"Already got a watch," he answered without looking back. He didn't know what Jackie's deal was, but he wasn't about to get involved.

Rae stuck out her tongue and peered into the bathroom mirror. The fungus-looking spot was still there, but she thought it was a little smaller. *It's nothing to worry about, anyway,* she told herself. *The doctor told you that.* She stared at her tongue another few seconds, then pulled it back in.

Maybe I should take a shower, she thought. She'd bought some new gel, aromatherapy stuff that was supposed to soothe and comfort. She could use both right now. Why had her dad forgotten the papers he had to grade at his office tonight? A night she definitely didn't want to be alone.

Rae picked up the tube of gel off the counter, then set it back down. There was no way she was going to relax in the shower right now, even if the gel was laced with Xanax or Prozac. How could she feel comfortable in the shower—naked—when Mr. Not-the-meter-man could be lurking around somewhere?

With a sigh Rae wandered out of the bathroom and headed to the kitchen. She opened the fridge and took out a muffin that Alice, their keeper, as she called herself, had made for her and her dad. Rae brought the muffin to her lips, then realized she wasn't hungry. She put the muffin back. The last thing she needed on top of everything else was to develop some kind of eating disorder.

She squinted into the darkness outside the kitchen window. Didn't see anything. Then headed into the living room. After Marcus had left, she'd started a sketch—another one of her mother, the only thing she seemed to be able to draw lately. She added a couple of lines, then tossed the pad down. Even though she was only about a quarter of the way done, she could tell her mother was going to turn out looking sick, sick and half crazed. Rae didn't need to see that.

If Anthony wasn't such a self-absorbed weenie, he'd be here with me right now, Rae thought. She crossed over to the living-room window and checked the front yard. Everything normal. At least everything seemed normal. It wasn't always easy to tell.

Marcus would definitely have stayed. *And he'd come back if I called him,* Rae thought. But he didn't know anything about what was really going on in her life, and she had no desire to tell him. Too many people knew already. Too many people were in danger because of her.

But Yana knows almost everything, Rae reminded herself. She didn't know Rae's mother had killed Rae's mom's best friend. And she didn't know about the fingerprint . . . thing. Rae still didn't know what to call it exactly. What, a *power*? A special ability? It's not like she was the new Wonder Woman or anything. It felt so weird to think of it that way. Which was exactly why she *wasn't* telling Yana. She didn't want her one good girlfriend to think of her as some sort of screwed-up comic book hero girl or whatever.

But Yana knows pretty much everything else. She'd understand why Rae was freaked, at least.

Rae hesitated, then hurried to her bedroom and hit speed dial three. Yana answered a few seconds later. "I'm going crazy," Rae blurted out as soon as Yana said hello. She even forgot her promise to Yana to avoid any of that crazy/insane lingo left over from her days at the hospital.

"Why? What's going on?" Yana demanded, ignoring the crazy reference—probably because she could tell Rae wasn't in good shape.

"Right this second? Nothing," Rae admitted, letting out a slow breath. "But yesterday I caught a guy in the backyard," she continued. "He said he worked for the power company, but I checked him out, and he was bogus. I keep trying to figure out who he is. If he's the same guy who was behind the pipe bomb and those nasty little presents I've been getting. Or if there's some new psycho who is interested in me for some completely different reason."

"Did you tell your dad?" Yana asked. "Not the whole thing, but just that there was someone in your yard who shouldn't have been."

Rae flopped down on her bed and covered her face with a pillow. "Huh-uh," she admitted. "He's not here right now. And even if he was, I don't want him to go into all-out worrying over me again."

"Add nine-one-one to your speed dial," Yana ordered, her tone brisk and businesslike. "If you see anything, *anything,* you get the cops over there." She paused. "I could come over, too, if you want," she added, her voice softening.

"No, it's okay," Rae answered. "There's really nothing going on over here. And my dad should be back soon. He just made a run to his office at the college."

"So is there something else going on?" Yana asked. "I mean, along with just the fake power company guy. 'Cause you said that was yesterday, but you sound like there's something, I don't know, still getting to you."

Rae shoved the pillow off her face. "I can't keep anything a secret from you, can I?"

"Don't know why you even try," Yana answered.

"Okay, here's the deal. I've been getting these weird numb spots," Rae admitted, leaving out the part that she got them after she touched fingertips with someone to pull out their thoughts. "Anyway, I got a look at my mom's medical records, and I think she might have had the same kind of symptoms. Remember how I told you she died in the hospital—"

"From some weird wasting disease," Yana finished for her.

"Yeah. I went to my doctor, but she has no clue what the numb spots could be," Rae explained. "And I'm starting to think it could be connected to—to whatever killed my mom." Rae stopped, leaving the implication of that idea hanging in the silence between them. "My mom was in this New Agey group," she continued when Yana didn't say anything. "And now I'm finding out that some other people in that group have died. So what if it's related somehow?"

"There's one way to know," Yana said. "We need to talk to anyone from that group that's still alive."

"Yeah, but I haven't found anyone," Rae said, the frustration building inside her. "I mean, I did find the daughter of one of the women in the group. Her mom died last year. She might have some info. Might. Or I could just be being delusional; you know, turning into one of those conspiracy theory freaks." Rae sighed. "I just hate to make this girl—Amanda Reese—go through being interrogated about her mother—"

"But you've got to," Yana cut in. "If she's your only source, you've got to."

Rae closed her eyes. "I don't even know how to start, what to say."

"You said you found her . . . so you know where she lives then, right?" Yana asked.

"Mmm-hmmm," Rae replied.

"Well, tomorrow we'll go there," Yana said. "We'll figure out what to say together. It'll be okay. We'll make it as easy on Amanda as we can, I promise."

Rae felt a small smile tug at her lips. At least she wasn't alone. She was so grateful to have Yana, someone she could count on. Especially since the list of people who fit that description was getting shorter all the time, now that Anthony was too busy impressing Jackie Kane and the rest of Sanderson Prep to care what was happening to her.

Chapter 5

Anthony rubbed the back of his neck, feeling for a tag. That was the last thing he needed— to go walking into his first Sanderson Prep party with a friggin' tag hanging off him. That'd be the same as announcing that he'd gone out and bought new clothes so he'd look nice. Absolute humiliation.

Get the hell in there, Anthony ordered himself. He pulled in a deep breath and strode up the front walkway, but he hesitated outside the front door. He didn't belong here. New clothes or not, he just didn't belong here.

You're being such a weenie, he thought. *You were invited. Now, go.* He jerked open the door and stepped inside. Now what? Now where should he go?

A bunch of people were dancing in the living room—to a sound system that probably cost more than his mom's car. Didn't matter. Anthony definitely wasn't going to attempt dancing—or asking anyone to dance.

Kitchen. Safest bet. He picked a direction and headed off, trying to look purposeful. *Just going to get myself a beer, everyone. See how well I fit in? I know all about parties.* He nodded at the people who looked familiar, but didn't slow down. Bad things could happen if you slowed down.

He passed the long line leading to one of the bathrooms—in a place this size there must be, man, at least three—then spotted another crowd farther down the hall. Spillover from the kitchen. Had to be. He inched his way inside and over to the keg on the closest counter. Some of the tension seeped out of his muscles when he saw a bunch of guys from the team gathered around it.

"Fascinelli, you're just in time to hear what a loser Salkow is," Sanders called. Anthony relaxed a little more. What had he been so wigged out about? Clearly they wanted him here.

"Yeah, Salkow's trying to get his old girlfriend back, and she's not having it," McHugh added. "And the girl's a total nut job. She spent the summer in a mental ward, and Salkow still can't score with her."

Anthony's hands curled into fists. It took a conscious effort to shake them loose, but he managed it.

"Rae's not a nut job," Marcus defended, his eyes flashing. "Just shut up."

"I agree," Ellison told Marcus. "She turned down the chance to come to the party with you. That's a sign of extreme mental health. Now, if it was me she turned down, 'nother story."

Anthony filled a plastic cup with beer to have something to do with his hands other than throwing punches. These bozos had no idea what Rae had gone through. *And it's not your job to explain it to them,* Anthony thought.

"What does she want from me, anyway?" Marcus asked. He drained his beer and squeezed the plastic cup until it splintered.

"Has she seen the size of your package? 'Cause if she has, that could be your problem right there," Sanders answered.

Anthony took a swig of his beer but had trouble getting it down. Had Rae seen—had she and Marcus— *None of your freakin' business*, he told himself.

"If she hasn't seen it, maybe you could start stuffing," McHugh suggested. "Or there are those pump things—"

Marcus bounced his cup off McHugh's head. "I'm serious. I want her back, and I'm getting nowhere."

Anthony mumbled something about checking out the pool table—he didn't even know if there was one, but it seemed like the kind of house that would have pretty much all the rich-guy toys—and pushed his way out of the kitchen. He liked Marcus and everything. But that didn't mean Anthony was going to listen to him bitch and moan about how much he wanted to get in Rae's pants. *Get back together with her,* he corrected himself.

He could see it. Could see them as a couple. Rae and Marcus. Marcus and Rae. Prom queen and king and all that bull. And as much as he didn't want to admit it, he'd seen the look in Marcus's eyes when his friends cut on Rae. The guy really did care about her.

A rhythmic chant started up from deeper in the house, and Anthony followed the sound, wanting some kind of distraction. As he got closer to the sound, he could make out the words of the chant. "Jack-ee, Jack-ee, Jack-ee."

The chant got louder as he entered a room with, yeah, a pool table. A tight circle of people had formed near the double doors leading to the backyard. They were all leaning down, staring at something on the floor. Some of the guys were practically drooling, and a couple of girls looked repulsed.

Got to see this, Anthony thought. He elbowed his

way into the circle. The first thing he spotted was a halo of blond hair. He tilted his head and saw—big surprise—Jackie. She had a funnel in her mouth. Some guy Anthony had never seen was pouring vodka into the funnel, and Jackie was sucking it up like she'd learned to breathe the stuff instead of air.

Christ, Anthony thought. *She probably only weighs about a hundred and ten. How is she still even conscious?* Nobody seemed too worried about it. The chant grew frantic. "Jack-ee, Jack-ee, Jack-ee." Anthony couldn't take his eyes off her as she arched her back, raising her head up to meet the vodka stream pouring into the funnel.

"New record!" someone shouted. Jackie held up one hand, and the guy pouring reluctantly stopped. The crowd let out a long cheer, and Jackie smiled. She licked the end of the funnel, getting the last few drops of the vodka and earning herself another cheer.

So this is how the other half parties, Anthony thought. If he'd seen Jackie walking down the street, all perfect hair and polished-rich-girl thing, he'd never have imagined her like this, lying on the floor, vodka slamming. Never imagined her shoplifting, either.

Jackie pushed herself to her feet and grinned. "Baby just kicked some butt," she cried. Her eyes locked on Anthony, and a second later she had her arms wrapped around his neck. She backed him through the crowd, pushed him against a wall, and started kissing him. His mouth tingled from the traces of vodka on her tongue.

What the—? What? Me? Anthony was incapable of completing a thought. But whatever was going on here felt way too nice for him to stop it. He licked her bottom lip, then his tongue was brushing against hers.

"Can't believe Jackie would—" he heard a girl say.

"Hey, Marcus, Fascinelli's getting some." The words sounded like they were coming from the end of a long tunnel. "Maybe you should forget about Rae and go for Jackie."

The sound of Rae's name brought her face into Anthony's mind so clearly that he jerked away from Jackie. "Oh, no, you don't. I'm not done with you," Jackie said. And her hands were on his back, pulling him back to her.

Rae wants nothing to do with you, remember? Anthony thought. *She doesn't even want to be around you in her freakin' school.* He wrapped his hands around Jackie's waist, feeling a little stretch of soft, warm, smooth skin, and deepened their kiss until his whole world was all sensation, no thought.

"Jackie, hey, Jackie!" The words forced their way

into Anthony's head. He wasn't sure how much time had gone by. Could have been a minute. Could have been an hour. "Jackie! Want to try to break the tequila record?"

Jackie wriggled away from Anthony. "I don't want to try—I want to do it!" she exclaimed. She started toward the vodka guy, who was now the tequila guy.

Anthony snagged her by the elbow and leaned close so that only she could hear what he had to say. "Mixing is going to make you sick as a dog," he told her. "And you've probably had enough of everything."

Jackie gave him a little shove away. "Just because we exchanged saliva for a few minutes doesn't mean you get to start telling me what to do." She spun and stalked off, leaving Anthony standing there like a complete idiot.

"This is the address," Yana announced as she pulled up in front of one of the Victorian houses in Little Five Points, one of the houses that had been carefully refurbished.

"I still have no idea what to say to her," Rae said. "I can't just ring the doorbell and go, 'Hi, I want to ask you a bunch of personal questions about your dead mother.' "

"You could try pretending you're the Avon lady,"

Yana said. "Yeah, it could really work. First we'd have to get some truth serum," she continued, getting into it. "And we'd mix it in with some foundation. Then we give the Amanda girl a free makeover. The serum seeps into her bloodstream through her face, and she tells us everything we want to know."

Rae laughed, and some of the tension building inside her crumbled. "Really, though, what am I supposed to say?" she asked. "I'm trying to think what would get me to talk to a stranger about my mom, and there's nothing. It's not as if I even talk to my friends about it."

"Yeah, we only talked about her, like, one time," Yana agreed.

"And that was because I trusted you," Rae said. "You'd seen me at my absolute worst in the hospital, and you still were actually willing to talk to me." Rae still remembered how amazing it felt when she realized Yana wasn't just being her friend because it was part of her job as a hospital volunteer.

"So Amanda needs to trust you," Yana said.

"Yeah, tonight," Rae answered. How impossible was that?

She and Yana sat for a minute in silence. "It seems like the only way to do it is to tell her the truth," Yana finally said. "Not all of it, not the part about you maybe being sick—that would freak her way out. But you both have moms that are dead. You want to know more about yours. She'd probably get that."

Rae unfastened her seat belt. "Okay, you're right, you're right. Count of three, we just go up there. And the right words will . . . they'll come to me. Somehow." She opened the car door halfway. "One, two, three." Rae forced herself out of the car and slammed the door behind her. *The girl's mother has been dead a year,* she thought as she headed for the front door. *The scab has probably just started to really form, and here I come to rip it off. But what choice do I have?*

Before she could think too much more, Rae reached out and knocked on the door. A girl a few years younger than Rae answered, only opening the door partway. "Um, hi, are you Amanda Reese?" Rae managed to ask.

The girl didn't open the door any farther. "Yeah. Well, but everybody calls me Mandy."

"Mandy, okay," Rae said. "I'm Rae. And this is my friend Yana. I don't know if you remember, but I called you a few weeks ago—"

"You're the one who called and asked for my mom." Mandy's eyes began to glitter with unshed tears. *Oh God,* Rae thought. *Oh God. Worst nightmare here.*

Rae's mind raced frantically. *Just do what Yana*

said, she thought. "I think your mom and my mom might have known each other," Rae said, her throat tightening. "I . . . my mother's dead, too. And I've been wanting to find out more about her. I thought maybe you'd be able to help me, that maybe your mother mentioned—"

The tears that had been glistening in Mandy's eyes started spilling down her cheeks. She made an awful choking sound as she tried to get control of herself. "Go away. Please just go away," Mandy managed to get out. "I can't talk to you."

Chapter 6

"Jack-ee, Jack-ee, Jack-ee." The chant grew softer, almost inaudible, as Anthony slid the glass door closed behind him and pulled in a deep breath of the cool night air.

A moment later the glass door was pulled back open. "Jackie's funneling tequila," someone shouted, and most of the guys who'd been splashing around in the pool with their clothes on headed inside.

"Don't know what antibitch drug Jackie's been taking, but I like it," one of them said as he passed Anthony. Anthony shook his head. The girl was going to be hugely sick—not that it was any of his business, as she'd pointed out. *Like I really wanted to stick around and hold her hair while she puked,* Anthony thought. He walked around the pool—the freakin' pool—sidestepping the couples making out on the lounge chairs. He needed a few minutes by himself before he could deal with the party again.

"Fascinelli," someone called. Anthony squinted and saw Marcus leaning against one of the magnolia trees near the back fence. Reluctantly Anthony headed over to him.

"Hey," he said, wondering why Marcus was hiding out.

Marcus took a long pull on his cup of beer. "Do you know Rae?" he asked abruptly. "Rae Voight."

Crap, Anthony thought. Talking about Rae with Marcus was not his idea of a party. It was more like his idea of hell. "I think I've seen her around. We're not in any classes together," Anthony answered. He didn't know if Rae had told Marcus that she was in group therapy. If she hadn't, he wasn't going to be the one to do it.

"Well, what do you think of her?" Marcus asked.

"She's cute," Anthony said. "Do you think the Sabertooths—"

"Cute?" Marcus repeated. "You think she's cute? That's it? She's an artist, you know. Did you know that?"

He's trashed, Anthony realized. "Like I said, I've just seen her around, so—"

"She's much more than cute," Marcus continued.

"The guys—they don't get it. They think *I'm* psycho to go for some psycho girl when I was with Dori. You know Dori?"

Anthony shook his head. "I don't know that many people yet." He glanced around the dark backyard, hoping he'd spot someone from the team he could call over. If he found Marcus someone else to talk to, then Anthony could cut out. But he didn't see anyone he knew.

"Dori's beautiful, okay? And when I was with her, she was always doing stuff to make me happy. Little presents. That girlie, you know . . ." Marcus took another swig of beer or tried to. Anthony figured out his cup was empty before Marcus did.

"But Rae. Rae's . . . *Rae*. The other guys don't get that. They're like, 'You're whipped, Salkow. Just shut up already. You can have any girl you want.' They just don't get it." Marcus leaned toward Anthony, so close, they were almost touching noses. "But you get it, don't you?"

Anthony moved back a step. "Yeah. Want to go back inside? Get a refill?"

Marcus leaned back against the tree trunk and slowly slid down it until he was sitting on the grass. "I want her back so bad. But I don't deserve her."

Anthony scanned the yard again. There had to be

somebody here who could get him out of this friggin' confessional. But no.

"I hurt her, man. I really hurt her." Marcus grabbed Anthony by the knee, and Anthony squatted next to him, torn between pitying the guy and wanting to pulp him. "I *hurt* her." His voice came out all quivery.

Crap, Anthony thought, *any second now he's going to be bawling.*

Little spurts of guilt kept going through Rae as she looked at Mandy's tear-stained face. *You can't give up now,* she told herself. She placed her hand lightly against the door—

*/Cocoa Krispies/*nothing ever works/stay home sick again/

—not trying to hold it open, just trying to get Mandy to reconsider. "I know it's hard," Rae said quickly. "My mom died practically right after I was born, and it's still hard for me to talk about it. A year—a year, that must feel like nothing."

Mandy pulled in a deep, shuddering breath and wiped the tears off her face with her sleeve. "Sometimes," she admitted. "And sometimes it seems so long ago that I can't even really remember her face all the way, or, you know, how her voice sounded."

Keep her talking, a calm, cold part of Rae

instructed. But she didn't want to coax Mandy toward going deeper into the pain. It wasn't right.

"You have pictures, though, right?" Yana jumped in. "And probably even videos."

"Yeah, but it's not the same," Mandy answered.

"Of course it's not the same," Rae said, shooting Yana an abort-the-mission look. There had to be some other place to get the information she needed.

"My sister practically has this shrine in her room," Mandy confided, opening the door a little wider, although not wide enough to be an invitation to step inside. "Pictures and clothes and perfume. It's kind of sick. I just—I couldn't even sleep with all that stuff around me. Em—that's my sister—keeps saying if I don't pick some stuff out of what's left, she's taking it all."

"You should have a couple of things," Rae told her. "You don't have to have them out. You don't even have to look at them—don't ever if you don't want to. But someday you might get the urge, and if you do, there should be a box in a closet somewhere waiting for you. I have one."

Rae pictured the cardboard box of her mother's things that her dad had in his closet. Five years ago she would have wanted to burn the stuff if she'd had the chance. Forget five. Even a year ago. But now . . . now Rae was starting to understand a little about her mother. And although what her mother had done horrified Rae, she had to accept that learning everything about her mother was essential to staying alive herself.

"Maybe you're right," Mandy said.

Rae had gotten so deep in her own thoughts that for a moment she had no idea what Mandy was talking about.

"She's definitely right," Yana answered. "If you want, we could help you."

You're pushing her too hard, Rae thought. But to her surprise, Mandy swung the door open wide. "Actually, yeah, that would be good," Mandy told them as Rae and Yana came inside. "I don't want to do it alone, but my sister or my dad . . ."

"Yeah, I wouldn't want to look at my mom's stuff with my dad. I know I'd start getting all worried about how he was feeling," Rae said.

"Did your dad . . . did it take him a long time to—" Mandy closed her eyes for a long moment, then opened them. "To get back to normal?"

Normal. Such a funny word.

"I remember him being normal when I was a little kid, doing all the dad stuff," Rae answered. "But really, I don't know how well he was coping. He's okay now, though, I think. Sad sometimes. But okay, too."

Mandy nodded. Her face looked tight, like she was struggling to keep her expression from cracking. "Okay, so, I guess we should get started," she finally said. She started fiddling with her long, light brown hair but didn't take one step. "Maybe you'll find out what you wanted to know when we look in the boxes. You thought there was some group our mothers were in together, right?" Mandy asked.

"Uh-huh. Some New Agey kind of thing. I hardly know anything about it," Rae said. *Except that some- one in prison knew about it,* Rae thought, a little shiver running through her as she remembered touch- ing that fingerprint on the basketball the prisoners had been playing with. And that someone was dis- turbed—no, frightened—that Rae might have been born while her mother was in the group. "Did your mom ever mention it?"

Mandy shook her head, then she started making a thin braid in a section of hair near her face.

She's getting scared, Rae thought. *She's going to back out.*

"How did your mother die?" Mandy suddenly blurted out.

She'd rather do anything than face whatever is in those boxes, Rae thought. *Even ask questions about my mom.*

"She . . . the doctors weren't really sure," Rae

answered slowly. "It was like her body was somehow turning against itself, destroying itself. They couldn't figure out what was happening or how to stop it before it was too late."

Mandy shuddered. "That sounds terrible," she said. "I'm sorry." She paused, still carefully braiding her hair. "With my mom it was even faster," she said, her voice shaky. "She was on the way back from the store, and these guys, these guys jerked her out of the car at a red light and shot her. Then they stole the car." Mandy blinked rapidly. "She would have given them the car. I know she would have."

"Bastards," Yana muttered.

"Yeah," Mandy said. "And we got the car back, anyway. They killed her for a car, and the cops ended up getting it back from them. It's out in the garage under this sheet. It's like a ghost. I don't even go out there unless I have to." She undid the braid seconds after it was finished, pulling at it so hard, Rae was afraid she was going to rip the hair right out of her head.

"Come on. The stuff's in my sister's room." She turned on her heel and led them down the hall, past the living room, past the kitchen. She stopped in front of a closed door. "My sister hates it if I go in without asking."

"Is she here?" Rae asked, surprised. The house

had an almost empty feel. She'd assumed Mandy was the only one home.

"No." Mandy gave a nervous laugh. "So I guess it's stupid to worry about it." She slowly turned the doorknob, then pushed the door open so hard, it banged against the wall. "Don't know my own strength," Mandy mumbled as she led the way inside.

God, it is like a shrine, Rae thought, taking in the little bouquets of dried flowers on the dresser and the dozens of photos of a woman who was probably around Rae's dad's age. Each photo had a little candle stationed next to it. The air held the fragrance of the candle wax and of recently burned incense.

Rae's heart constricted as she thought about what it would be like to lose her father. She'd never known her mother, but her dad . . . he was like air, a constant, essential thing in her life, even if she didn't think about him that way most of the time.

"The boxes are under the bed. Let's take them to my room," Mandy said. Rae could see why she was eager to leave. The room was beautiful, but it was creepy, too.

"Can we help you carry them?" Yana asked, already heading for the bed. She was in extreme pushy mode, definitely borderline obnoxious, but Rae was glad she was there. If Rae and Mandy were alone, they could end up frozen in place forever. At least that's how it felt.

"Okay," Mandy told Yana. "It's the two flowered boxes."

A second later Yana was on her knees. She pulled one of the boxes free and handed it to Rae—
/why?/shouldn't have/why?/why?/

—then grabbed the other one and stood up with it cradled in her arms. "Lead the way," she told Mandy.

"My room's kind of a sty," Mandy admitted as she walked them over to a closed door a little farther down the hall. With an embarrassed half smile, half grimace, she opened the door.

Mandy's room didn't smell like incense or candles. It smelled like . . . pizza. Rae tracked the odor to a pizza box almost buried under a pile of dirty clothes. Mandy wasn't exaggerating about the state of her room. There were piles of junk on every flat surface—except the bed. It was a peaceful island in the middle of the chaos. "I guess I'll just put this here," Rae said, setting her box at the foot of the bed. Yana placed her box next to Rae's.

"Sorry about—" Mandy made a helpless gesture.

"Hey, makes me feel at home," Yana said. "You should see my room."

Rae was pretty sure Yana was lying, remembering the row of flowers Yana had planted along her front

94

walkway. But lie or not, it worked. Mandy sat down cross-legged in the middle of the bed, patting spots on either side of her. Rae and Yana took the invitation, then silence began to fill the room like cold water.

Mandy just kept staring at the boxes, and the quiet began to feel like a weight on Rae's shoulders, on her chest.

"How should we do this?" Yana asked, the silence sucked down the drain at her words. "Rae and I could hold stuff up and you could tell me keep or not keep—unless it would be weird for us to touch the stuff."

"No. No, that would be good," Mandy answered, starting a new little braid.

That was lucky. Rae hadn't even thought about what she'd do if she couldn't get a chance to touch the objects and pick up whatever thoughts she could.

Yana gently removed the cover from the box closest to her. She pulled out a pink sweater, beaded with a snowflake pattern.

"Not keep," Mandy said quickly. "She hated that one."

"For the not-keep pile," Yana told Rae, handing her the sweater. Rae noticed that the tag was still on it. She ran her fingers lightly across.

I prissy thing! what was he thinking!

The rest of the sweater had a few fuzzy, grief-soaked thoughts. Nothing else. Rae carefully set it down.

Yana pulled a gray zip-front sweatshirt out of the box. The front pocket had come loose on one side, and the tie was missing from the hood. Mandy reached out and took the sweatshirt, then brought it to her face and pulled in a long, deep breath. "Keep," she said, her voice muffled. Reluctantly she handed the sweatshirt to Rae.

/smells like my/

That thought was so clear, it had to be Mandy's. There was more fuzzy grief, probably from whoever packed the box, but there were many more happy thought fragments, fragments about dogs chasing sticks, tide pools, kids splashing. *Beach vacation,* Rae figured.

Yana pulled out another sweater. Mandy shook her head. "This is the only piece of clothing I want." She took the sweatshirt away from Rae and tucked it under one of the pillows on the bed.

Rae started to tell her that the smell would last longer if Mandy kept the sweatshirt wrapped in plastic, then changed her mind. That sweatshirt should be touched, not turned into an artifact.

"Just more clothes in this one," Yana said. "You sure you—"

"Yeah," Mandy answered, patting the pillow the sweatshirt was nestled under. Rae returned the pink sweater to the box, letting the old thoughts roll through her. Yana firmly replaced the lid.

"Okay, next one," Rae said, sliding the other box over in front of her. She shot a glance at Mandy to make sure she was doing all right. All right as she could be, considering, Rae decided. She took the lid off the second box and removed the first item—a miniature red toy car with two little men in it, one blond, one with dark hair.

I loved Hutch! leave it out to!

A giggle almost escaped Rae's lips as the playfulness in the thoughts zigzagged through her. She covered with a cough.

"Keep or not keep?" Yana asked.

"Not keep," Mandy said, her voice a little too loud. Rae set the car aside and removed a deck of tarot cards.

I knew! a power? I almost always know! I should go? I never touching again!

Emotions came with the thoughts, flickering through Rae strobe light fast, almost too fast to recognize. There was pride, excitement, curiosity, fear, apprehension, confidence—and fear again, more intense than anything else Rae picked up off the deck.

"Was your mom into the tarot?" Yana asked. Rae was glad Yana had. Right now she was too overwhelmed to speak.

Mandy shook her head. "She said all that stuff, psychic stuff, was bull. Those cards can't have been hers. They must have gotten in the box by mistake."

Rae put the deck into the not-keep pile. She knew the cards had been Mandy's mom's—the thoughts on the deck had the same flavor as the happy ones from the sweatshirt, the annoyed ones from the tag of the pink sweater, the silly ones from the red car. Rae knew something else, too—there was a time when Mandy's mom believed she had a power—a power to know things from the cards.

"Maybe she used to be more into stuff like that," Rae suggested. "The group she was in with my mom was supposed to be New Agey. Tarot cards are New Age, kind of."

"No, she really hated all that stuff," Mandy insisted. "I remember this one time when I was little. We had a big fight because I wanted to see a fortune-teller at my school carnival, and she said no. I had a fit." Mandy stared past Rae, her eyes blank. "I remember I told my mom I hated her."

"Who hasn't said that to one of their parents?" Yana asked before silence could pour into the room again.

Rae dropped the cards and grabbed a half-finished sock puppet—a cat, at least it looked more like a cat than anything else.

I ten thumbs! gonna buy something!

A burst of impatience and frustration popped

through Rae. Making the cat had not been fun, fun, fun.

"Keep," Mandy said. "I remember when she was making that. Trying to make it," she corrected herself. Mandy held out her hand, and Rae gave her the puppet. Then Rae reached into the box again, touching something smooth and cool.

I Melissa!

Rae's fingers convulsed when her mother's name and a stab of concern entered her through a fingerprint. Slowly Rae withdrew the item—a Polaroid photo of a group of women. Near the center was Rae's mother. Standing next to her, arm around Rae's mother's shoulders, was Erika Keaton. The woman who had been her mother's best friend. The woman her mother had murdered.

"Keep or not keep?" Rae heard Yana say, although it sounded like she was talking from a couple of rooms away. Fingers trembling, she searched the photo for more prints.

I can't see any of them again! Melissa and Erika should! sick! why did!

Rae felt the photo being tugged out of her grasp. She tightened her grip.

"Rae?" Yana asked, still sounding far away.

"My mother," Rae managed to get out. "She's in this picture."

"It must be of the group," Yana said. She leaned over to get a look. "The sign they're standing around

99

says Wilton Community Center. Is that where the group was held?" She took the picture from Rae and looked at it more closely. "Weird," she said. Her voice was so quiet, Rae could barely make out the word.

"What?" Rae asked, scooting closer. She took the picture back and studied it.

"No, it's just weird to see your mom," Yana said. "I'd never seen a picture of her or anything, but she—she looks like you."

"I don't think I was even born when this was taken," Mandy said, peering over Rae's shoulder. "No wonder I don't know anything about the group."

"I just need—is there a bathroom I can use? Something I ate is totally turning against me," Rae said, words tumbling over each other.

"Right across the hall," Mandy answered.

Rae bolted. As soon as she got inside the bathroom, she locked the door, then sank down on the edge of the tub. The feelings from Mandy's mother were still slicing through her, sharp as broken pieces of a mirror.

Disgust. Revulsion. Anger. Terror. Urgency.

Whatever Amanda Reese had experienced in the group had left her with a hatred of it. And a fear so strong that she never wanted to see anyone from the group again, not even her friends. And Amanda had been friends with Rae's mother; Rae had felt that in the thought. She'd been friends with Erika Keaton, too.

Rae flipped over the photo and saw that a list of names had been carefully printed on the back. *Got to write them down,* she thought. She opened the medicine cabinet and found a lip liner that would work as a pen, then pulled the instructions out of a box of tampons for paper. Carefully she copied the list.

Suddenly Rae had a lot more leads. But would any of them take her where she needed to go?

Anthony walked to the quickest exit—the back-yard gate—finally free of Marcus and his sniveling. Some of the other guys had shown up and taken him inside to check out the bathtub they'd filled with beer.

"Jack-ee, Jack-ee, Jack-ee," he heard as he swung open the gate. What now? Was she seeing how much rat poison she could down?

He veered toward the crowd gathered on the front lawn. He didn't exactly want to look, but he couldn't stop himself. A blaring car horn jerked his attention to the street, and he realized that the car was what everyone was staring at—the car with Jackie behind the wheel.

"I'm going to break the all-time world speed record,"

she yelled from the lime green convertible. "I'm going to go so fast, you're not even going to see me."

And they're all watching this, like they're waiting for somebody to pass out the popcorn, Anthony thought, disgusted. At least Jackie wasn't going fast. Not yet. She was weaving down the street, getting extremely close to some parked cars, but she wasn't in danger of really hurting herself. Not yet.

Anthony trotted around the crowd, heading for the car. "Hey, Jackie, want to take me for a ride?" he called.

Jackie shook her head hard, the car mirroring her movements. "You don't deserve to get that close to me," she yelled. The morons in the crowd gave an ooooh. Was there even one of them who realized that if Jackie did start slamming on the gas, she could end up paralyzed? *Or dead.*

At least the top's down, Anthony thought. He locked his eyes on the passenger seat—and leaped. He landed on his stomach, halfway in and halfway out, the metal of the window frame biting into him. Jackie put on the gas. Not too much, just enough to attempt to jerk him free. Probably to the alcohol-soaked sponge that was her brain, it felt like she was going a hundred miles an hour.

He grabbed the dashboard with one hand, the back of the passenger seat with the other, and hauled himself into the car.

"Get out!" Jackie screeched. He ignored her and reached for the wheel. She jammed her foot on the gas, flooring it. The car hurtled toward somebody's SUV. Anthony managed to wrench the wheel to the right in time to avoid a crash.

But they were going fast now. Way too fast. Anthony tried to get one of his feet under Jackie's so he could kick it off the gas. But he wasn't able to make the maneuver and still watch the road, which he needed to do before they hit a tree or something.

Jackie took the corner hard, tires squealing—and headed for the intersection. Clearly she didn't know or didn't care that they were flying toward a red light.

"I am *not* dying in this car!" Anthony yelled. Keys, he'd go for the keys. He jerked his body toward the ignition. Jackie took one hand off the wheel and tried to claw him away. They were five feet from the intersection. Three feet.

Anthony managed to catch Jackie's flailing hand in one of his own. Then he turned off the ignition and jerked the keys free. "I want to go fast!" Jackie yelled as the car came to a stop.

"I'll give these back to you tomorrow," Anthony said, wrapping his fist around the keys. He shook his head. Why had he wanted to come to this stupid party in the first place?

Chapter 7

Rae tried to pay attention to Ryan Lardner. But God, he defined *monotone*. What had Jesperson been thinking, assigning Ryan the part of Othello?

She shot her English teacher a glance and found his gray eyes looking right back at her. As usual. Or at least it felt that way. It was almost like Jesperson thought of Rae as his only pupil, teaching his class just for her. He called on other people, yeah. But he didn't look at any of them the way he looked at her.

He just wants be like teacher of the year or something, she told herself. *He's new at Sanderson, and he just wants to prove how great he is. His mission isn't just to stuff Shakespeare into our heads, he wants to understand us, help us with our problems, have us come to him with our deepest secrets.*

Us. Us, right, Rae thought. *Don't you really mean me? He wants me to come to him so he can help me through all my teen angst, my poor-little-girl-who-had-a-breakdown garbage.*

Rae again tried to focus on the words Ryan was saying—anything to keep from thinking about Jesperson, freak-of-the-year candidate. But God, didn't Ryan realize what he was actually saying? It was like he was seeing each word as . . . as a *word*, with no larger meaning. Didn't he get that Othello was talking about how he was planning to kill his wife? It's not like she expected Ryan to be a great actor. She was no actress, and she was reading Desdemona. But come on. He could bring a little something to the party.

" 'She wakes,' " Ryan read.

Time to see if you can do any better, Rae thought. " 'Who's there? Othello?' " she read. At least they came out sounding like questions. Her voice actually went up where it was supposed to.

Ryan began his next line but was interrupted by the door swinging open. One of the office ladies came in and handed Jesperson a note. He read it quickly. "Ryan, you're needed in the office. Take your things with you."

The class gave the obligatory soft "ooooh." But no one thought that Ryan was really in any kind of trouble. Ryan's personality was as monotone as his reading voice. It was hard to imagine him doing anything the least bit out of the ordinary. Although wasn't it always the guys like that who blew?

"We don't have too much time left," Jesperson said. "I'll just read Othello for the rest of the scene."

Oh, great, Rae thought. Her face went hot as she found her place. " 'Will you come to bed, my lord?' " she read, keeping her eyes on her book.

Jesperson walked down the aisle toward her, reciting the next line, not even reading it, which meant he could look at her the whole time. He leaned down, bracing his arms on her desk. Rae got out the answering line, managing not to squirm.

Jesperson leaned even closer, close enough for Rae to get a whiff of his sweat. " 'If you bethink yourself of any crime unreconciled as yet to heaven and grace, solicit for it straight,' " he recited. And he was antimonotone. His voice was charged with passion and an undercurrent of fury.

Rae couldn't help herself from leaning away from him as she read the next line. Jesperson didn't let up. As he—Othello—began to speak of killing her—Desdemona—his eyes seemed lit from within. She struggled on. There were only a few more minutes of class, and then this creepy interlude would be over.

But the few minutes stretched out, feeling double or triple their actual length. And with each second that passed, Rae felt more tense, her hands tight on the sides of her book, her ankles clamped around each other. Othello/Jesperson got more threatening. More menacing. And now he was making his move—

"Don't touch me!" Rae cried out, and the whole class laughed.

Jesperson straightened up and backed away a step. "Guess I'm a better actor than I thought," he said. He smiled at Rae, an oily smile she could almost feel against her skin. "You didn't think I was really going to smother you, did you?"

"Of course not," Rae said, her voice coming out sharp when she'd wanted it to sound light and jokey. To her huge relief the bell rang. She jammed her copy of *Othello* in her backpack, snatched up her purse and jacket, and jumped out of her seat.

"Can I talk to you a minute, Rae?" Jesperson called when she was halfway to the door. Reluctantly she turned around and walked over to his desk.

"I just wanted to make sure you were okay," he said, his voice pitched low so only she could hear. "That scene seemed to really get to you."

"Well, it *is* about murder," Rae answered.

"Even so." Jesperson rubbed the dark stubble on

his chin, the stubble that half the girls in class thought was so sexy. "Is there anything bothering you? Anything you're feeling anxious about? You know you can talk to me anytime."

"Nope. You're just too good an actor, Mr. Jesperson, that's all," Rae said, forcing herself to meet his gaze steadily. "Got to go grab lunch." She hurried from the room without waiting for a response. There had only been a couple of other people left, and Rae absolutely had not wanted to be alone with Jesperson for even a few minutes.

I must stay in control. I must be patient. My hands are shaking to smother Rae, to put a pillow over her face and hold it there until her body goes limp. Or pick up a knife and slash her open. Or put a few drops of poison in her food, poison that is slow to act, not fast, something that would make her suffer. I never want to see her face again. I never want to hear her voice.

My thoughts are filled with murder. When will I do it? Where? How? But I must stay in control. I cannot let her grow suspicious. She is afraid, I can tell. Her fear is all over her face—it is in her voice. I must be patient. If I am not, I will never find out who else is so interested in Rae Voight. I must get this information before I make my move. The time for the murder will come. Soon it will come.

* * *

Anthony stood in front of the cafeteria, turning Jackie's car keys over and over in his fingers. He wanted to give them back to her out here without an audience. There was no reason to remind everyone else of how out of control she'd gotten at last night's party.

He snorted. Not that anyone was likely to forget. He gave the keys an extra-hard flip, and they went flying out of his hand and skidding across the floor. He followed them—and spotted Rae coming down the hall. A kicked-in-the-gut feeling immediately followed the Rae sighting.

It's better that she didn't let you spit out an invitation to the party, he told himself. He'd heard way, *way* too much about Marcus and Rae's deal last night, but one thing that had really sunk in was that Marcus sincerely cared about the girl. And he was so much more her, man, her type, or whatever you wanted to call it.

Anthony crouched down and picked up the keys, staying low for a few extra seconds in case Rae wanted to breeze on by without having to acknowledge him. Probably be the best thing if she did.

"Hey, Anthony." Anthony stopped staring at the keys, lifted his head a little, and found himself staring at Rae's legs. He'd recognize them anywhere.

"Hey," he said back as he straightened up. "So

you, uh, feeling better?" He took a quick look down both ends of the hallway. It took him a second to realize he was checking for Marcus. Like he needed Marcus's permission to talk to Rae or something. Which was bull. They weren't even together anymore.

But he wants them to be, Anthony thought. *They should be.*

". . . except for this really nasty rash and the pus, I'm doing okay," Rae was saying when he tuned back in.

"Huh?" Anthony said before he realized she was messing with him. What a moron.

"Forget about it," Rae answered. "I'm fine. See you." She started to turn away.

"Wait," Anthony blurted out. "There's something I wanted to ask you."

Rae turned back to face him and raised one eyebrow, waiting. *Crap. Now what,* Anthony thought. He didn't really have anything to ask her, he just wanted her to stay. Only for a second. Then he wanted her to go. He just didn't want her to go all pissed, which he could tell she was because he'd blinked out when she was talking to him.

Nervously Anthony twirled Jackie's key ring around one finger. "Um, yeah, I was wondering how well you know Jackie. Jackie Kane."

"We used to hang out," Rae answered. If anything,

the annoyance in her eyes had gotten more intense. She really didn't want to talk to him a second longer than she had to. "But it's been a while."

"I'm kind of worried about her," Anthony admitted. "At the party she was out of control. And I was just wondering if she was always like that."

Rae folded her arms across her chest. "That's what you wanted—to ask me about Jackie?"

Anthony nodded. Didn't she hear what he'd just said?

"Okay, well, let me tell you about Jackie since you're so interested. Last year, back when we were friends, Jackie was the antithesis of wild."

Antithesis. Thanks, Rae. Wasn't there a freakin' longer word you could have used?

"She was eye on the prize—you know, doing everything to have the perfect high school record to get into the best school and everything," Rae continued. "That's almost all she cared about."

"Well, she's definitely changed, then," Anthony said. "Last night she drank enough to make five guys puke. And—"

"Look, I want to work on one of my paintings during lunch. Was there anything else you wanted from me?" Rae asked, her voice sharp.

Anthony shoved his hands in his pockets. Now that he was thinking about it, there was something

Rae could do. "Maybe you could do a little"—he lowered his voice—"a little *research*. You know. 'Cause I think something might be going on with her, something danger—"

"Jackie can take care of herself, okay?" Rae interrupted. "I have to go." She practically ran off.

Anthony shook his head, unable to pull his eyes away from the hall Rae had stalked down, even though she'd already turned the corner. What was her deal? Why was she suddenly acting like he was the last person on the planet she wanted to be around? Yeah, he knew he wasn't up to Marcus's level or anything, but weren't they kind of friends or whatever?

"Are you planning to give those back to me?" Oh, great. Anthony recognized the voice—Jackie. And she didn't sound like she was in any kind of better mood than Rae was.

"Yeah, I'm giving them back," Anthony said as he turned toward her and tossed her the keys. She looked like crap—as much as a girl like her ever could look like crap. There were dark hollows under her eyes, and her makeup couldn't quite hide the unhealthy yellow color of her skin.

"Thanks," Jackie muttered, then she headed toward the caf.

Thanks. That's it. Like he was hired help or something. Like she hadn't had her tongue practically down to his stomach last night. Anthony caught up to her with two long strides. "You're welcome, princess," he told her. "You should take it easy on the drinking and driving. Even you wouldn't look good splattered across a street somewhere."

Jackie grabbed him by the arm and pulled him into the little space next to the drinking fountain. "Let's get one thing clear—you don't know me," she told him. "You do not know anything about me. You don't have the capacity."

"I know what I saw last night—" Anthony began.

"Shhh, shhh, shhh." Jackie pressed one finger against his lips. "Let me give you a little advice. Don't talk. You're cute. And you're a novelty here, which is an advantage. But when you talk—" She crinkled up her nose. "You lose whatever appeal you have. Now, run along and have fun while you're still the interesting new boy and not just a loser from Fillmore who happens to be able to throw a football."

Anger swelled up in Anthony as he reeled from her words. "Fine," he bit out. "Trying to do you a friggin' favor, but fine." Anthony strode toward the gym. There was no way he could go into the cafeteria and eat at the usual table with Jackie sitting across from him. Not now that he knew she thought of him as this huge pile of crap.

He passed a couple of guys from the team and

gave them a half salute. *Are they thinking the same garbage Jackie is?* Anthony wondered before he could stop himself. *Am I just this big, dumb football-playing bear to everyone?*

Self-absorbed jerk, Rae thought as she entered the empty art room and slammed the door behind her. Well, tried to slam—it was one of those doors that always closed really slowly.

No, make that Jackie-absorbed jerk, she corrected herself. She grabbed her big white painting shirt off its hook and pulled it on. She couldn't believe Anthony was all worried about Jackie. *Jackie.* Had someone tried to kill Jackie? No. Had someone kidnapped one of Jackie's friends to get information about her? No. Was Jackie possibly dying of some freaky incurable disease because she had a psychic power? That would be no again. But *she* was the one Anthony was worried about.

Rae still hadn't gotten a chance to tell him about the non-meter-reader guy. Or her numb spots. He hadn't stopped talking about Jackie long enough for her to get a word in.

Well, screw him, Rae thought. She didn't need Anthony. She and Yana had the situation completely under control.

Paint. You're here to paint, she reminded herself.

Her portrait of her mother was almost done. She'd been working on it like a fiend, getting in some time before school, after school when she could, and every day during class. It's like she was compelled to work on it, even though painting her mother was usually the last thing she'd want to do.

Rae headed toward her easel, passing the row of little cubbies along the wall. Out of the corner of her eye she caught Jackie's name on one of them. She wasn't in Rae's class, so she must be in one of the beginner ones. Rae hesitated. Was there something wrong with Jackie? Rae herself had seen Jackie shoplifting, something Jackie would have been completely scornful of last year.

I could just do a quick sweep, Rae thought, already wiping the wax off her fingers with a paint-stained rag. She reached out and swished her fingertips back and forth over the cover of Jackie's sketchbook.

/don't tell/tuna/wouldn't blink if I/don't mention/nice perspective/pointless/why even/secrets/new guy/can't talk to/no one cares/

Rae absently rubbed the spot just under her rib cage. She felt like a hole had opened up inside her, and the emptiness ached. *That ache isn't in you,* Rae reminded herself. *It's in Jackie.*

Anthony was right. Something bad was going on

with her, so bad that Jackie believed that everything was pointless and that no one cared about her. Rae figured it had something to do with whatever those secrets Jackie had were. The *don't tell,* and *can't talk,* and *don't mention* were probably all about . . . whatever the secrets were.

Maybe I could talk to her, Rae thought. *She obviously really needs to talk. Except, God, Jackie and I have hardly talked at all since I got out of the hospital—just a little polite chitchat, and even that felt strained.*

Besides, now that Anthony had moved Jackie to the top of the list of girls to save for the week, she'd be fine, right? And what could Rae really do? It's not like she'd want to talk about all her deep, dark stuff with Jackie, and Jackie would probably feel the same way about her.

Rae sighed as she continued over to her easel. She slid off the sheet covering her canvas—and felt like all the blood had been drained from her body.

Her mother's face . . . Rae forced herself to really look at it. Acid, she decided. Acid had been splashed all over the painting, eating ragged holes in her mother's face. And then the canvas had been slashed with a knife.

Rae backed away until she hit the sink behind her. She leaned against it, her legs feeling too weak to support her. She looked at the painting again, and from this distance she realized that the slashes weren't random. They formed words—*Stop asking questions*.

Stop asking questions. That meant someone knew that she was at Amanda's last night. Rae turned around, fumbled with the cold-water knob, and managed to turn it on, then she leaned forward and let the stream of water run over her face.

"Okay," she muttered as she straightened up. "So someone doesn't want me to ask questions." She pulled a couple of rough brown paper towels out of the dispenser and scrubbed her face hard, her hands shaking. Whoever it was, they had been here again . . . in her school. In her *art* room. They had touched her painting, ruined it. But they were scared, too, she realized. They didn't want her to ask questions because she was getting close to the truth—finally.

"Well, it's going to take more than this to stop me," she said out loud, fighting to keep her voice strong. She stood up straight and faced the painting again. "A lot more than this."

Chapter 8

Rae felt like a squirmy five-year-old as she waited for group therapy to end. Every second that went by was a second she couldn't use to find out the truth about her mother. Every second that went by was a second Rae might desperately need to save her life.

Come on, come on, come on, she thought as a new girl—Rae couldn't even remember her name, and the girl'd said it about three minutes ago—stammered her way through a tour of her psychosis. Rae reminded herself how hard it was to learn to spew personal stuff in front of strangers and tried to give the girl an encouraging smile. But she couldn't make her lips move that way.

Come on, come on, come on, she thought. *You're*

the last one. When you're done, we're done, even if it's a few minutes early. Rae had called Yana after school and filled her in on what happened to her painting. Before Rae could even go on, Yana had jumped in and said they should go straight to the Wilton Center, today. So she was picking up Rae from group, and then they were heading over.

Finally the girl talking came to an abrupt halt. *Thank God,* Rae thought. But then Ms. Abramson, the group leader, asked the girl a question. Of course. Because that was her job. Getting them all to dig deeper, look harder.

Rae realized her heel was tapping rapidly against the floor. She pressed her hand on her knee to force her foot flat to the floor and keep it there. Things like that—unconscious repetitive motion, or signs of anxiousness, or signs of lack of social awareness—could and would all be noted in her chart. And if she wanted to stop coming to this bizarre fun fest, she had to make sure she was so normal, she put people to sleep.

"Okay, that's it for today," Ms. Abramson said. Rae managed not to leap out of her chair and whoop. Instead she stood up quietly, like a normal person, put on her jacket, like a normal person, gathered her stuff, like a normal person, and walked out of the room, like a normal person.

She was only a few steps down the hall when Jesse Beven caught up to her. "Shouldn't we be doing *something?*" he asked, his blue eyes intent on her face.

"Doing something?" Rae repeated.

"Yeah, doing something," Jesse said. "You know, to find out—" He took a moment to check that no one was listening. "To find out who kidnapped me and who tried to *kill* you. Are we going to come up with some kind of plan? Or are we just going to keep sitting around with our thumbs up our butts?"

Rae knew Yana was probably already waiting for her in the parking lot. But it was clear Jesse wasn't going to let her go without some kind of answer. "I want to do something, yeah, of course," she told him. "But we've got nothing, remember? The guy who kidnapped you is long gone, and we have no idea who hired him. Or who hired David Wyngard to set that pipe bomb. How can we come up with a plan when we've got nothing?"

Jesse's frown deepened into a full-fledged scowl, and his eyes darkened.

"Has something new happened?" Rae asked. "Are you worried—"

"I keep having nightmares, okay?" he blurted out. "I'm back in the warehouse and—whatever." He avoided her gaze, and she noticed his hands clenching into fists at his sides. "Every time I wake up, I'm pissed off. I'm not letting whoever did that to me get away with it."

Rae nodded, worried that Jesse wasn't so much pissed off as terrified. But she wasn't going to ask. That was a Ms. Abramson kind of question.

"If anything happens, anything that would give us a starting place, you're gonna be the first person I tell," Rae promised him, feeling a little spurt of guilt. Finding out the truth about her mom could end up leading her to the person she and Jesse both wanted to find. But she didn't know that for sure. If she did get any info that Jesse would want, she'd . . . well, she'd decide what to do then. "I've got to go, okay?" she said.

"You better not be getting all momlike and trying to protect me," Jesse told her. "This isn't just about you."

Rae nodded, biting her lip. Momlike. Ha.

Jesse started off down the hall.

"Jesse," she called out without actually deciding to. His name just sprang out of her mouth.

"Yeah?" He turned to face her.

You don't need to know this, she told herself. But she asked the question, anyway. "Um, do you know where Anthony was—I mean, do you know why he wasn't in group?"

You shouldn't care, she thought. *You don't need*

Anthony Fascinelli. But the image of acid eating through the painting of her mother's face wouldn't leave her. And even though Anthony had shown zero interest in what was going on with her lately, he was the person she wanted to tell what happened.

"Oh, right. You were a little late. Abramson announced that he isn't coming anymore. I guess he's going to be checking in with her by himself," Jesse explained. "The group was going to get in the way of his football practice, and skipping practice would mean losing his scholarship."

Jesse didn't sound like he thought losing the scholarship was such a bad thing. *He must feel like he's losing Anthony, his almost big brother,* she realized. This was the main place they saw each other. "I'm sure you'll still see each other," Rae said.

"Whatever," Jesse answered. He walked away without another word, clearly not wanting to have some mini-therapy session with Rae about his feelings over the Anthony sitch. *You need to go, anyway,* she thought. Time. Going. Tick, tick, tick. She started power walking down the hall but only got about five steps before Ms. Abramson fell in beside her.

"Rae, I just wanted to talk to you for one minute," Ms. Abramson said.

"Sure," Rae answered, even though she wanted to scream. Ms. Abramson steered her over to one of the benches that lined the hall. "What's up?" Rae asked as they sat, wanting to get the conversation started so it could end.

"I noticed you were a little agitated in group today," Ms. Abramson began.

Rae rolled her eyes, disgusted with herself. Then she immediately worried that Ms. Abramson had seen the eye roll and thought that Rae was giving her attitude.

"I, yeah, you're right," Rae answered. "I don't know why. Ants-in-the-pants syndrome."

Ants-in-the-pants syndrome? Had that actually come out of her mouth? Good thing extreme dorkishness wasn't a sign of mental illness, or Ms. Abramson would be bundling Rae off to the hospital.

"Those metal chairs aren't exactly comfortable," Ms. Abramson answered.

Is that it? Rae thought.

"But sometimes an issue will get raised in group that strikes a chord," Ms. Abramson continued.

Of course that's not it. What was I thinking? Rae asked herself.

"Sometimes you don't even realize what's happening. It can express itself as simply feeling uncomfortable or anxious," Ms. Abramson said. "Try to remember when you first started getting that ants-in-the-pants sensation."

"I had it before I even got here," Rae answered. Which was true. It had started up right after she got the stop-asking-questions warning. No big psychological mystery there.

Ms. Abramson studied her for a moment. "Did anything unusual happen at school today?"

"Not really. Just . . . typical school stuff," Rae told her, being careful to make direct eye contact. That was important to Ms. Abramson. She looked back at Rae, as if she thought if she stared long enough, she'd pull out everything in Rae's brain.

Rae liked Ms. Abramson, liked her more than any of the other therapists that she'd had to deal with. But God, sometimes it felt like Ms. Abramson wanted to peel her like an onion, stripping away layer after layer. And what would be left, that's what Rae always wondered. 'Cause with an onion? There was basically nothing there once all the layers of skin were pulled off.

"Typical school stuff," Ms. Abramson repeated after she'd finished the soul-searching look. "Okay, well, I just wanted to check. Oh, and I also wanted to schedule another of our individual meetings. How about after group next Monday?"

A question that wasn't really a question. Rae stifled a sigh. "Sounds good." The only answer she could give.

"All right, then. Enjoy the rest of your day," Ms. Abramson said.

Rae stood up and normal-walked until she was out of the building. Then she sprinted over to Yana's Bug and climbed in, breathless.

"To the Wilton Center," Yana said as she started the car.

Rae gave a halfhearted *whoo-hoo*. She'd been counting down the seconds until she could actually get out of the Oakvale Institute, where the group was held. But now that she and Yana were heading toward the center, it was like Rae could feel acid splashing on her own face again and again.

I could do it, she thought. *I could stop asking questions. I could—*

I could die. That was the alternative.

Rae scrubbed her face with both hands. "You okay?" Yana asked.

"Me? Could not be better," Rae answered, her voice coming out a lot more sarcastic than she intended it to.

"All righty, then," Yana said. She flipped on the radio, and they both listened to the music until they arrived at the Wilton Center, the place where the group had been held, the group that had Mandy's mother, Rae's father, and that basketball-playing prisoner so freaked out.

"It looks . . . extremely normal. From the outside, at least," Yana observed.

"Yeah." Rae climbed out of the car, taking in the clearly kid-made masks in one row of windows and the clearly adult-made whirligigs on the center's front lawn. Her eyes came to rest on the sign to the left of the whirligig display, and she felt like someone had slid an ice cube down the back of her shirt. The sign looked exactly the way it had in the picture of her mother and the other people in the group. "My mom was standing right over there," she murmured.

Yana grabbed her arm. "Let's go inside."

"Your hands are freezing," Rae complained as Yana towed her toward the main entrance.

"Well, I'm a little scared," Yana admitted, tightening her grip on Rae. "I've never told you this before . . . but people who knit? I find them disturbing."

"Is it the needles?" Rae asked. " 'Cause they are kinda big and pointy."

"No. It's not the needles. Or the yarn. It's the *people*. The people, I tell you," Yana said. "They want everyone to be just like them. They won't rest until we're all knitting woolly socks." She lowered her voice to a whisper. "It's a cult."

"Okay, we'll avoid them," Rae assured her, trying not to laugh as they stepped inside.

"It's even more normal looking in here," Yana commented.

"Mmm-hmmm." The walls were painted a soft yellow, the floors were covered in speckled linoleum, the air smelled like paint and paste and—Rae took another sniff. Like books. Lots of books. In the distance she could hear a string quartet rehearsing. And it sounded like there was flamenco dancing going on right overhead. "I guess all the classes are in the middle," she said. There wasn't a person in sight.

"Which makes this the perfect time to look around," Yana replied. She started down the hallway to the right without letting go of Rae. A few of the doors they passed were open, but all she saw was more *normal*. A group of women making a quilt. Some little kids watching a puppet show. Some people doing yoga.

The sign outside is the same, Rae thought. *But everything could have changed inside. It's been almost twenty years. Maybe there's nothing here to find. Maybe—*

"Let's try back there," Yana said, pulling Rae away from her thoughts. She nodded toward a door with a sign that said Wilton Staff Only.

Rae glanced over her shoulder. The hallway was still empty. "Okay. I think we've seen enough up here."

"Yeah. I'm about to go into a diabetic coma. This place is even nicer than wherever it is they live on 7th *Heaven*," Yana answered as she led the way to the door.

"Haven't seen it," Rae admitted.

"You're not missing anything," Yana said. She pulled open the door. Rae peered over her shoulder. All she could see was a narrow stairwell leading down.

Yana hesitated for half a second, then started down the stairs, heading for the tiny landing. Rae pulled the door shut behind them and followed her. The smell of paint and paste grew fainter, overpowered by the scent of some industrial cleaner. They must have switched bottles halfway through mopping the stairs because Rae was getting a blast of pine and lemon. Not a nose-friendly combo.

Rae switched over to mouth breathing, the sound of her breaths loud in her ears. But there was something else. Another soft sound. Rae grabbed Yana by the elbow. "Stop a second," she whispered. She held her breath. The soft sound continued. What was it?

Sneakers, she realized. Sneakers on the cement stairs below them. Heading *up* toward the landing they were heading *down* to.

Rae and Yana exchanged a look, then they both turned and ran back up the stairs. Rae tried to stay on her toes, but one of the chunky heels of her shoes came down on the edge of one of the steps, and the sound echoed through the stairwell.

Yana reached the top of the stairs, grabbed the doorknob, and jerked. "It's locked," she whispered, twisting the knob back and forth.

"Can I help you ladies?" a friendly voice called.

Rae and Yana turned around, and a forty-some-thing guy with one of those old-guy little gray pony-tails climbed the stairs toward them. He didn't look pissed off or anything.

"We were just . . . trying to find the darkroom," Rae blurted out. "I was thinking about taking a pho-tography class here." *Please let them give photogra-phy classes,* she thought. "And my friend is interested in knitting," Rae added, ignoring Yana's snort.

"You're heading in the wrong direction," the man answered. He reached the door, pulled out a key ring, and let them back out into the main hallway. "I'm Aiden Matthews," he said. "I'm one of the instructors here. I'd be happy to give you a little tour. And I know just the place to start." He led them to the end of the hall and around the corner. "What do you think?" He gestured to a glass case filled with knitted sweaters. "A couple of sessions and who knows—we could be displaying your work out here," he told Yana.

"Cool," she muttered.

Okay, you've got a chance to get some facts here, Rae thought. *Use it.* "I was wondering, how long have you worked here?"

"I started here right out of college, if you can believe that," Aiden answered.

He could have known her, Rae thought, a mix of excitement and apprehension rolling around inside her. "Really? Wow. You must have been here when my mom was taking classes," Rae said. "It was almost twenty years ago. Before I was born. Obviously, right. I know she really liked this place. She made a lot of friends here."

Stop, Rae ordered herself. *Too much. Too much.*

"What's your mom's name?" Aiden asked. "Maybe I'll remember her."

"Melissa Voight," Rae told him, watching his face. His eyes widened slightly, but that was his only reaction. "Actually it wasn't a class, exactly. Some kind of a group, a New Agey thing, my dad said."

"Uh-huh, uh-huh." Aiden glanced down the empty hall behind him, looked back at Rae and Yana, then checked the hall again.

Talk about your ants-in-the-pants syndrome, Rae thought. *He looks like he wants to run out of here and never stop. What does he know?*

"I'm teaching a class that starts in a few minutes,"

Aiden said. "It . . . it slipped my mind when I said I'd give you a tour. I'll have to ask you to leave because it's against our rules to have nonmembers wandering around unescorted. But if you want to give me your addresses, I'll send you some info on the knitting and photography classes."

What class starts at twenty minutes after the hour? Rae thought, glancing at her watch. Aiden clearly wanted to get away from them and get them out of here. *He definitely knows something.*

Rae pulled a notebook and pen out of her backpack, letting her old thoughts rush through her without paying attention to them, and scribbled down her name, address, and phone number. "You can send me the info for both," she told him. The guy was acting weird. There was no reason to give him direct contact with Yana. "Can I call you if I have questions?" she asked.

"I don't know that much about those particular classes," Aiden said. "But if you call the center, the receptionist can put you in touch with any of our teachers. I know they'd be happy to talk to you." He checked his watch. "I really have to get going."

Rae stretched out her hand. It was time to get what she came for. "Thanks for showing us around."

Aiden grabbed her hand. His was damp with sweat, which made it easy for Rae to slide her fingers down until she and he were fingertip to fingertip.

Instantly it was like his thoughts were hers. Not just his thoughts. His memories. His fears. His emotions. Even the stuff he kept hidden from himself, buried deep in his unconscious.

Focus, Rae ordered herself. *You don't have much time.* There. There was an emotion cluster about hearing her mother's name—anger, fear, chased with nausea. Rae tried to stay with the emotions, and they led her to a tangle of thoughts.

how much does she know/and I showed her around/know about experiments/gonna get reamed/how she died/does she know/her mother/her mother/

Reluctantly Rae released Aiden's hand. She knew there was so much more she could have gotten from him. But not without keeping the fingertip-to-fingertip contact, which would make anyone suspicious. "Don't forget to send me the stuff. We're definitely interested in those classes," she told him.

And I'll definitely be coming back here, she thought. *Because Aiden—or someone else here— knows everything I need to know. I can feel it.*

"I won't," Aiden said over his shoulder. He was already halfway down the hall.

Rae led the way out of the building. "Well, that was a total bust," Yana said.

"Yeah," Rae answered, needing most of her concentration to keep walking to the car. Her knees were weak with fear—some of Aiden's, some of her own.

The word *experiments* kept ricocheting through her head. That word, it had felt almost . . . almost *evil* when she pulled it out of Aiden's mind. What kind of experiments was he thinking about? And were they done on Rae's mother?

Chapter 9

Anthony dressed quickly and headed out of the locker room after Friday's practice. He wouldn't have minded a little time in the steam room—how unbelievable was it that he went to a school that had a steam room—but he didn't feel like hanging out with the other guys.

Because, you wuss, you got your feelings hurt by that little miss rich girl yesterday. How pathetic is that? It was completely pathetic. It was also true. Even with the guys on the team, the guys who'd welcomed him to the school—after he'd kicked their butts on the field—the guys he'd partied with, little snatches of what Jackie'd said kept going through his mind.

You're a novelty here, which is an advantage. Just

a loser from Fillmore who happens to be able to throw a football. Run along and have fun while you're still the interesting new boy. Don't talk. Don't talk.

It's all crap, he told himself. *It's just the ravings of one girl who got her panties in a bunch because you told her the truth—that she was acting like an idiot.* But Jackie's words kept whispering in his head.

Just a loser. Don't talk. Run along. Novelty. Have fun while—

"Hey, Fascinelli, wait up," Marcus called from behind Anthony, interrupting the loop of Jackie's voice. "There's something I want you to take a look at."

Anthony stopped and turned around. Marcus loped toward him, looking as friendly as a big blond golden retriever. *If he was just pretending to* accept *me or whatever, he wouldn't—* Anthony refused to let himself finish the thought. He was turning into a total girl, analyzing every friggin' thing. "Whatcha got?" he asked.

Marcus glanced behind him, then he pulled a long velvet box out of the pocket of his team jacket. "Keep this between us, okay? The guys are already ragging on me enough about Rae."

Rae. Crap. Why did it have to be about Rae?

Probably because you let him cry on your shoulder

over her at the party, Anthony answered himself. *Probably because you don't go around saying what a nut job Rae is. Probably because as far as Marcus knows, you've practically never even spoken to her.*

"No prob," Anthony said.

"Okay, so what do you think?" Marcus opened the box, and Anthony saw a thin little gold-link bracelet—a thin little gold-link bracelet with freakin' diamonds all over it. Or what looked like diamonds.

"Are those real?" Anthony blurted out.

Marcus laughed. "No, I'm trying to get Rae back by giving her fakes." His smile faded. "So do you think she'll like it?"

"Yeah," Anthony answered, thinking how he and Marcus might as well be from two different planets. "What's not to like?"

"Right. But lately with Rae, I don't know what to expect. It used to be that I was everything she wanted. Before we started going out, I'd see her looking at me, you know? And it was all over her. A lot of girls are like that—" Marcus shook his head. "I sound like such a jerk. But you'll see. Now that you're on the team and everything, girls will be doing anything to get your attention."

Yeah, right, Anthony thought. *Rae's been trying to climb me like a tree.*

"Anyway, like I said, Rae, she wanted to be with

me. I know she did. Practically all I had to do was smile at her, and that was it," Marcus said. "Right before she, uh, had her breakdown, we were getting real close to doing it, and—"

"But now?" Anthony interrupted, afraid he'd break out in hives if he had to hear any more. He liked Marcus. And he thought Marcus was the kind of guy Rae should be with. Marcus could give her freakin' diamonds, for chrissake. But he did not want to, could not, hear any more details.

"But now when she looks at me, it's like she's trying to decide something," Marcus answered. "Like will I mess up again. Sometimes we've had a couple of minutes where it felt almost like it did before. No, I'm lying. Where it felt like it could eventually be like what it was before." Marcus snapped the box shut and shoved it back into his pocket. "Do I sound whipped or what?" he asked, sounding disgusted with himself.

"Yeah, you do. I've been meaning to talk to you about it," Anthony joked, glad to have the bracelet out of his sight.

"It's sick," Marcus exploded. "Why do I even care? There are a whole bunch of girls who are giving me that look. All I'd have to do is say one word and—" He shook his head. "But it wouldn't be the same."

Marcus looked at Anthony, clearly waiting for some kind of advice. At the party it hadn't mattered what he'd said because Marcus was drunk off his butt. But now Marcus was looking for something real.

"You know, I'm not exactly an exp—" Anthony began, then he spotted Sanders and McHugh pounding toward them.

"You guys hear?" McHugh gasped out as he came to a stop next to Marcus. He didn't wait for either of them to answer. "They found Jackie passed out in the girls' locker room."

"They think she took a whole bottle of aspirin," Sanders added.

In the distance a siren began to wail. It grew louder by the second. *The ambulance coming for Jackie,* Anthony realized, his body going ice cold.

"The number you have reached has been disconnected. There is no new listing. If you believe you have reached this number in error, please hang up and try again."

Rae slowly hung up the phone, but she didn't try again. She'd already tried three times, hoping that somehow her fingers had slipped up and dialed wrong again and again. With a sigh she crossed the name Shelly Baroni off the list she'd made that night at Mandy's.

The list is getting pretty ragged, she thought. A lip liner pencil wasn't made for paper, although it might be an interesting addition to a painting. *I'll copy the list over,* Rae decided. She grabbed her sketch pad off her desk and impulsively pulled a calligraphy pen from the Monet mug she kept all her writing stuff in.

You're stalling, she told herself as she began to copy the names, using elaborate curlicues and loops. She didn't start writing the names more simply, though. Because she wanted to stall. She'd already tried to find five of the people on the list, and nothing. Nothing but disconnected phones, and new tenants who'd never heard of the person she was looking for, and, oh, yeah, the two people who weren't listed anywhere in Atlanta.

It's been almost twenty years. People move around. They get married. They get divorced. They—

They die.

Like Rae's mother. Like Mandy's mother. Like Erika Keaton. What if everyone on the list was dead? What if that's why she hadn't found even one of them?

"Hello, you're not living in *Scream VII* or something," she muttered. Well, except for the part where someone had tried to kill her. And the part where someone had sent her Erika Keaton's ashes. That had definitely been like something out of a horror movie.

Rae's hand shook as she started on the next name, and a blob of ink smeared across the paper. She ripped the page off her sketchbook, tore it in half, tore it in half again, and again, and again.

Then she froze, a chill washing up her back except for the large numb spot that had formed at the base of her spine after going fingertip to fingertip with Aiden yesterday. She'd heard a car pull into the driveway, and her dad wasn't due home for another hour at least. Rae hurried to the window and took a cautious peek out. "Anthony," she breathed when she spotted the Hyundai in the driveway.

She let the pieces of paper fall to the floor like confetti, not bothering to move over to the waste-basket, then ran to the front door. God, she was glad he was here. Yeah, she was pissed off at him. But even if all he did was talk about how amazing he was at football practice, he'd be in the house with her. She wouldn't be alone. And she'd feel safe. She always did around Anthony.

Rae pulled open the door just as Anthony was about to knock. He stood there, one hand raised, and stared at her in surprise.

"Were you expecting someone else?" Rae asked.

"No, I wanted to see you," Anthony said quickly. "I needed to tell you about Jackie."

Jackie. Jackie again? Rae was willing to listen to

stories of football glories or how annoying Anthony's brothers and sister were or pretty much anything else. But every time he brought up Jackie, she wanted to scream. How could he be so worried about Jackie when he knew Rae was in danger practically every second? "What about her?" Rae snapped.

"She's in the hospital," Anthony answered. "She overdosed on aspirin."

Rae closed her eyes. *I am the most selfish person in the universe,* she thought. *I knew something bad was going on with Jackie, and I was too worried about how she'd treat me to try and talk to her. That and too pissed off at Anthony. Let's be honest here.*

"I thought maybe you would—" Anthony began.

"Just let me get my jacket," Rae answered.

Anthony tried to keep his attention on the road, but he couldn't stop himself from shooting little glances at Rae. There'd been lots of other times that they'd been in the car together without talking, but this time felt different. It was like Anthony's throat was drying out, like pretty soon he wouldn't be able to talk even if he wanted to. Man, how had things gotten like this between him and Rae?

How? Let's see. You started going to her school, and suddenly she couldn't stand your presence for whatever bizarre reason.

Rae cleared her throat. Did she have that dry gritty feeling, too? Anthony rolled down the window. Maybe all they needed was some fresh air.

Rae cleared her throat again. "After we talked yesterday, I did do a fingerprint sweep of something of Jackie's," she said. She twisted her hands tightly together. "I should have done something right then. Her thoughts were all about no one caring and secrets, things she can't mention." Rae dropped her head back on the seat. "God, she might as well have thought, 'I'm going to commit suicide tomorrow.'"

"No. If it came across that strongly, you would have done something. I know you." Anthony reached over and touched her arm quickly, so quickly, he didn't know if she'd even felt it.

"Thanks," she said softly as they pulled into the hospital's parking lot. "Maybe there's still something of use we can do."

Anthony found a parking place, and they got out and headed up to the building. "So, uh, have you and Jackie, have you gotten close?" Rae asked.

"She pretty much thinks I'm a loser," Anthony answered.

"Then why—" Rae began.

"Same reason you're here," Anthony answered. "No one else is bothering to pay attention."

"I hate the smell of hospitals," Rae muttered as

the electronic door slid open and they stepped inside.

"Smells sort of like Oakvale," Anthony commented.

"Exactly," Rae said. "They all use the same industrial-strength cleaner. Just smelling it makes my heart start beating faster."

Being here is bringing back a lot of painful crap for her, Anthony realized. His gut reaction was to put his arm around Rae and pull her close to his side. But that wasn't their deal. Really, it never had been, except that in a few of their more extreme situations, they'd—

Jackie. Focus on Jackie, Anthony ordered himself. *That's why we're here.* He veered toward the reception counter. "We wanted to see Jackie Kane. She would have been checked in a couple of hours ago." It had taken Anthony a couple of hours to get himself over to Rae's.

The guy on duty tapped on his computer keyboard. "Fourth floor. Room 4010. She's allowed visitors, but don't stay more than twenty minutes."

"We won't," Rae answered. "We just want to make sure she's okay." She led the way over to the elevator, and they rode up in silence. Anthony wished he could think of something to say—his throat was drying out again—but what exactly he wanted to say to Rae Voight was way too complicated to figure out right now.

"It's this way," Rae said when the elevator doors slid open. She pointed to a sign on the wall that had an arrow indicating that rooms 4000 to 4020 were to the left. In less than a minute they'd found Jackie's room. The door was a quarter of the way open.

"Do we just, uh, walk in?" Anthony asked. He raked his fingers through his hair, his scalp suddenly itchy.

"Um, I don't . . ." Rae tapped lightly on the door. "Jackie?" she called softly. There was no answer.

Anthony gave the door a light push. His eyes went immediately to the bed. Jackie lay there, pale and still. The walls were bright yellow—so bright, her face looked even whiter in contrast.

"I don't want to wake her up," Rae whispered.

"I don't know. . . . Do you think she's conscious?" Anthony asked.

Rae let her breath out with a hiss, then stepped up to the end of the bed, studying Jackie more closely. "You're right. I don't think she is." She reached down and pulled open Jackie's chart, then swept her fingers back and forth across the doctor's notations. "They're feeling like her chances are good, though," she said, glancing back up at Anthony.

"Unless she does something stupid the second she gets out," Anthony muttered. He should have put a leash on her the night of the party and never let her off. His gut was telling him she was going to self-destruct, and he'd done the minimum he had to do.

"Let me see what else I can find out. If we know why she did this, that's the first step to stopping her from doing it again," Rae said.

Anthony watched her intently as she began to run her hands along the railing of the bed. Emotions that he knew weren't hers flickered across her face—condescension, worry, irritation, love, frustration, impatience.

Rae gently removed her fingers.

"Get anything?" Anthony asked.

She tilted her head from side to side, stretching out her neck muscles. "A little," she answered. "Mostly from her parents, I think. They're worried about her. . . ."

"But—" Anthony prodded.

"But there were a bunch of thoughts about Phillip," Rae said. She sat down in the plastic-covered chair next to Jackie's bed. "That's Jackie's older brother. I got stuff like, 'Don't we have enough to deal with already with Phillip?' "

"What's his deal, do you know?" Anthony asked, batting one of the balloons away from his head.

"I met him once at Jackie's, that's it. He's in boarding school now," Rae told him.

"Why? Was he getting out of control?" Anthony asked.

"No gossip about anything like that," Rae answered. "Phillip, from what Jackie said, was obsessed with getting into Yale. And that's the toughest school there is. I figured he just went to some outrageously exclusive prep school to get himself on the path."

"The path," Anthony repeated. "Right. And Sanderson Prep *isn't* the path to all that Ivy League bull."

"It can be," Rae said. "But you know, there's always a better school." She turned away from him and stared down at Jackie. "She would not be happy with people seeing her sans makeup."

"So, back to Phillip. It doesn't sound like he could be the thing pushing Jackie over the edge," Anthony said.

Rae frowned. "Except I did get all that stuff about secrets from Jackie's sketchbook. If something is wrong with Phillip, it could be something the Kanes don't want to get out. Some political aspirations there." Rae reached over and picked up Jackie's limp hand. "I'm going to see what I can get fingertip to fingertip."

She gently matched up her fingertips to Jackie's. Then Rae's head snapped back. Her eyes closed, and in an instant her body was heading straight for the floor.

Chapter 10

Rae tried to open her eyes, but she couldn't. If she could open her eyes, she knew she could stop them. But she couldn't. And they were coming for her, moving almost silently but with enough whispery, rustly sounds to signal their approach. Maybe she could pry her eyelids open with her fingers. All it would take was a slit, and they'd be gone.

But her arms wouldn't move. She couldn't get her hands close enough to her face. And they were coming. They were coming.

They were here.

Rae would have shrieked if her lips could open, if her lungs could pull in air. Instead she had to submit, silent, motionless, powerless, as the . . . the . . .

creatures—even without seeing them she knew they weren't human—gathered around her, pushing in closer and closer until they were like a second skin around her body and she could smell the sour breath they breathed out, the breath she was forced to breathe in.

"What do you want?" she cried. No. Tried to cry. The sound was only in her head.

Their hands—are they hands? Rae thought. She felt fingers, but they were thick and bristly. Their hands, or whatever they were, took hold of her, and she was suddenly aloft.

Open your eyes, she screamed, the words ricocheting through her head. But her eyelids seemed to be made of stone.

"Rae," a voice called in the distance. She knew the voice from somewhere. Somewhere a long time ago.

The voice rang out again. "Rae!"

Anthony, she realized. *It's Anthony.*

If she answered him, he would come, no matter where they were taking her. But her tongue was stone, too. And her lips. And the inside of her throat.

"Rae—"

Anthony's voice got fainter. She knew he was trying to tell her something, something important, something she could use to save herself. But the creatures were running, stealing her away from him, and his instructions reached her as random sounds that meant nothing

The creatures ran faster, Rae held aloft by dozens of hands, if that's what they were. She could tell from the way her body tilted that they were moving uphill. Then the creatures stopped in unison. Rae was passed forward along the row of hands, then hurled away. And she was falling. Endlessly falling.

Her body gave a jerk. Her eyes flew open. The first thing she saw was Anthony's face. "Wha— where?" she mumbled.

"We're in the hospital," Anthony answered. "In Jackie's room, remember?"

Saliva flooded Rae's mouth, and she swallowed. The simple reflex motion felt so good. Her body was her own again. She struggled to sit up, realizing she was lying on the floor cradled in Anthony's arms.

He tightened his grip on her. "Stay down for a minute," he ordered. "You were—I don't know what. It wasn't a seizure, but—"

"There were monsters," Rae mumbled, the words coming out garbled because her tongue and lips had somehow lost coordination. She waggled her jaw back and forth, stretched and pursed her lips, flexed her tongue, then tried again. "Monsters," she repeated, much more clearly.

"Monsters, huh?" Anthony brushed her hair off

her forehead. Her sweaty hair. How gross. She didn't want him touching it when it was like that. "What were the monsters doing?"

When he said the word *monsters,* Rae was hit by how ridiculous it was. She glanced around, her eyes taking in the sterile hospital room and Jackie's bed. Jackie. The last thing she could remember was touching Jackie's fingertips with her own.

"Maybe because Jackie was unconscious," she murmured as the realization sank in. "Could I have connected with her unconscious somehow? Except that wouldn't mean monsters. Maybe she was dreaming, and I got into it. Or—"

"Shut up for a minute, will you?" Anthony asked, his voice gentle. "Just shut up and keep still until you're sure you're okay."

Rae stared up at Anthony, trying to do what he said. But now that she wasn't in babble mode, she was hyperaware of how close their bodies were. Her head was resting on his thigh, and even through the denim of his jeans she could feel the warmth from his skin soaking into her cheek. His arms around her were like new ribs, a part of her own body. And she could feel his breath fluttering her hair. She was probably even breathing in a little of the air he breathed out. Rae sprang to her feet, overwhelmed by the unexpected intimacy.

She stumbled slightly, feeling a wave of dizziness.

"Are you sure you should be up?" Anthony stood, too, and studied her. "You look a little wobbly." He grabbed the pitcher of water off the table next to Jackie's bed, poured her a cup, then pressed it into her hand.

/GOTTA DO SOMETHING/SHE'S OKAY/WATER/PALE/

Anthony's fear mixed with the fading fear Rae already had going on, and his relief joined hers. She took a sip of the water, even though she didn't really want it, because it would make him feel better. She couldn't help feeling a strange sense of déjà vu, recalling that time at Oakvale after the pipe bomb when she'd gotten those same thoughts off a cup of water Anthony had given her. He was always there somehow when she needed him most. In fact, he must have caught her when she passed out, or else she'd probably be dealing with one major headache right now.

"Sorry I dragged you into this," Anthony said. "I didn't know—"

"It's okay," Rae interrupted him. "Stuff like this is what I should be doing with my . . . whatever. God, if I had done something after I did that sweep at school, Jackie might not even be in the hospital. I could have—"

"Just because you have this thing, this gift,"

Anthony interrupted, "it doesn't mean you're supposed to take responsibility for the whole world."

Rae smiled. "Oh, right. I forgot. That's your job."

Anthony glanced over at Jackie. Rae followed his gaze. "Let's come back tomorrow," she said. "I'm not going to be able to get anything from her that'll help. Not until she's conscious."

And until I can stop shaking, Rae thought, although there was no way she'd let Anthony know just how much that connection with Jackie had taken out of her. She didn't really want to think about it too much herself.

The phone rang. It sounded louder than usual, shriller. Rae rolled over in bed and snatched up the receiver, ignoring the old thoughts that tumbled through her mind. *Who's calling in the middle of the night?* she wondered as she mumbled hello. Then she realized sunlight was pouring in her bedroom windows. It was already Saturday morning. Obviously yesterday had taken even more out of her than she'd realized.

"Hello," Rae said again, her sleepy brain taking in the fact that there had been no reply to her first greeting.

"Rae. I'm calling for Aiden Matthews."

Rae sat straight up, heart jittering in her chest. It

was a woman's voice. Why was this woman calling about Aiden?

"You met Aiden—" she began to continue.

"At the Wilton Center. I remember," Rae interrupted.

"Yes. You had a lot of questions. He wanted to answer them. But he couldn't. Not there."

"Can he answer them now?" Rae asked, her voice coming out way too squeaky to sound human.

"Aiden would like to meet you face-to-face," she replied. "He didn't even feel it was a good idea to call you himself, which is why I'm doing it for him. He'll be waiting for you at the Motel 6 on Sherman. Room 212. No one will see you there."

Before Rae could ask another question, the dial tone began to hum in her ear.

It could happen today, she thought, hanging up the phone. *I could find out everything today.*

Or Aiden, your good friend Aiden, who you talked to for, like, half a minute, could have a whole other agenda planned, a little voice in her head warned. *I mean, we're talking Motel 6.* And so what if it was a woman who'd called her? Maybe she was in on it—Rae had heard of some crazy couples like that.

Rae grabbed the phone, getting her old thoughts again, and punched Yana's speed dial number. "I do not take calls before noon on Saturday," Yana mumbled when she picked up.

"Some woman just called and said she was calling for Aiden Matthews," Rae explained. "He wants a meeting. He—"

"I'm picking you up. I'm already there," Yana answered, then slammed down the phone.

Clothes. Need clothes, Rae thought. She climbed out of bed and had to grab the edge of her nightstand to keep from landing on the floor. Her right foot—it was numb. Completely. Toe to heel.

"It's never been this bad before," Rae whispered, every muscle in her body tightening. *Maybe it's because Jackie was unconscious,* she thought. *Or maybe, maybe whatever it is that's happening to me is speeding up.*

Stop, Rae ordered herself. *Just stop until you hear what Aiden has to say. He could know exactly what's going on. He could even know the cure.*

She walked to the closet, keeping her eyes on her feet. Watching her right foot seemed to make it work, even though she couldn't feel it.

Rae pulled out the first sweater and pair of pants her fingers touched, then yanked them on. She jammed on her sneakers, not bothering with socks, and rushed out of her room, still watching her right foot, willing it to move.

In the hall she made herself try to walk with her head up, and it worked okay. *See, you're doing fine,* she told herself. "Dad, I'm going out with Yana," she called.

"Okay, have fun," he answered from the bathroom. Rae knew he'd be in there at least an hour. He never left until he'd finished the crossword puzzle—in red pen—and given himself a grade based on how many squares he'd messed up.

She started to swing by the kitchen, then decided if she ate, she'd probably puke the food back up. Her stomach seemed to think it was riding a roller coaster.

Aiden better explain everything about the experiments, Rae thought as she rushed out of the house. That word—*experiments*—had been popping up in her mind ever since she'd pulled it out of his thoughts.

Had her mother and the other people in the group been experimented on? That was going to be her first question. Rae peered down the street in the direction Yana would be coming from. No sign of her.

Of course not, she thought. *It takes at least twenty minutes to get here from her house. Okay, maybe twelve the way Yana drives. And she had to get dressed and everything, too.*

I'll count to a thousand, she told herself. *By the*

time I get there, she'll be here. Rae hadn't done the count-to-a-thousand thing since she was a kid. But it had gotten her through some hard stretches of time—like the hours between when she woke up and when it was okay to wake her dad up on Christmas morning.

"One Mississippi, two Mississippi, three Mississippi," she began.

At six hundred Mississippi she heard the squeal of tires. A moment later she saw Yana's yellow Bug slamming around the corner. Three seconds later Rae was in the passenger seat. "Motel 6 on Sherman," Rae instructed. A second later they were off.

"Finally we actually get a *Charlie's Angels* assignment," Yana said with a grin. "None of this looking at old yearbooks. Or talking to sad little girls. Meeting a mysterious man in a hotel—that's more my style." Yana gave her short hair a little flip. "I get to be the Drew Barrymore angel 'cause she was the coolest. You should be the Lucy Liu one 'cause she was the rich, spoiled, prep school one."

"I'm not spoiled," Rae protested. She wanted to add that she and her dad weren't that rich. But to Yana they were, so Rae kept her mouth shut.

"You know, he might just be waiting there to get ahold of your young, ripe, jailbait flesh," Yana warned.

"Yeah, I thought of that," Rae said. "I'm not an imbecile. That's why you're here."

"We can kick his butt if he gets out of line," Yana answered, sounding like she kind of hoped he would. She started humming the *Charlie's Angels* theme song and didn't stop until they pulled into the motel parking lot.

"Park near the stairs. He's in room 212," Rae said.

Yana quickly found a space, and they climbed out. Yana started up the stairs with much hair flipping and posing with a pretend gun. "Come on, Rae. Show me your stuff."

Rae gave her hair a little toss, then trotted up the stairs, passing Yana. She was way too eager to find out what Aiden had to say to fool around playing games.

Yana caught up to Rae in the hall, and they walked down the faded green carpet side by side. When they got to room 212, the door was slightly ajar.

"Aiden," Rae called. "It's me."

No answer.

"Hello?" Rae gave the door a little push. A hand grabbed her by the wrist and jerked her inside. Immediately a blindfold was wrapped around her eyes. "You scream, you die right here," a rough voice told her.

Rae clamped her teeth together, but she couldn't keep a high, long whimper from escaping as her hands were tightly bound together. Whoever was doing this to her—Aiden? It didn't sound like him—was wearing gloves, so she couldn't pick up any information.

"On the floor, blondie," another voice ordered from the back of the room.

Oh God, they have Yana, too, Rae thought. The gloved hands pushed her down on a bed, and her feet were tied together. "Now, be a good girl and keep quiet. We'll know if you don't."

Rae heard footsteps move toward the door, then the sound of it opening and closing. She shivered as the door was locked from the outside.

Chapter 11

Anthony pulled into Rae's driveway, parked, and got out of the car. Rae wasn't one of those girls you could honk for. At least not in front of her house, when her dad was home and everything. He headed to the front door and rang the bell. *Hope her dad doesn't answer,* Anthony thought. The guy was decent. Anthony even liked him. But he was a professor, for chrissake. What did Anthony have to say to a guy like that?

The door swung open, and there stood—you got it—Rae's dad. He held a book in one hand, with his finger holding the place. Reading on the weekend. How disturbed was that?

Mr. Voight smiled. "Anthony, hi."

"Hi," Anthony said back. Was he supposed to

make some chitchat before he asked for Rae? "Uh, what are you reading there?"

"The new Stephen King," Mr. Voight answered. "The other professors in my department like to pretend they don't even know who he is. Even Rae doesn't know I read King. She'd say if I got to read junk like that, she should be able to watch TV. But I like his style. It's so immediate. His narrators, it really does feel like they're talking right to you. Are you a fan?"

"Not really," Anthony said, not bothering to mention that he hadn't even read one of the guy's books, even though he'd seen a bunch of the movies and thought some of them were cool. *Maybe in a few months I could try one of them,* he thought, surprising himself. *I mean, I am getting better at the reading stuff.*

"I guess you're here for Rae and not for a book club meeting," Mr. Voight joked. "Yana picked her up a few hours ago. I don't know when they're due back, but you're welcome to wait if you want to." He gestured inside with his book.

"She didn't leave a message for me or anything?" Anthony asked. He knew the answer before Mr. Voight shook his head. If Rae'd left a message, her dad would have already given it to Anthony.

Well, great. Yesterday he'd thought—it was

almost like how things used to be between him and Rae. But now Rae was ditching him after making plans to go see Jackie—Anthony realized Mr. Voight was still standing there, watching him. "Thanks, but I gotta get going," he said. He turned around and hurried back to his car, got in, and slammed the door so hard, the Hyundai shimmied.

So, I'll go by myself, Anthony thought as he backed out of the driveway and pulled onto the street. He and Rae had talked to a nurse on the way out of the hospital yesterday, and she was almost positive Jackie would be conscious by now. Which didn't mean she'd be happy to see him. He'd be willing to place a large bet that he wasn't anywhere on her list of approved visitors, even way at the bottom.

He slowed down a little until he was heading toward the hospital at about five miles under the speed limit. *If she has other people with her, that's it, I'm done,* he thought. *But if she's alone . . . if she's alone, I'll go in and talk to her. I don't know what I'll say, but I'll talk to her. At least for the five seconds it takes her to call me a lowlife and get security to escort me out.*

Slow as he was driving, Anthony eventually made it to the hospital. He parked as far away from the entrance as he could to buy himself a few more minutes. *Weenie,* he thought. He climbed out of the car, gave the door another slam, and headed into the hospital. He spotted a pay phone when he got to the row of elevators.

All right, Rae, let's see what's so important, you took off without even bothering to call me. Had to get in some mall time, probably. Yana was always dragging Rae off to the mall. Not that he heard Rae complaining all that much. Anthony fished a quarter out of the front pocket of his jeans and dialed Rae's cell phone number. The voice mail picked up.

"Rae. It's Anthony," he said. "We had plans today, remember? I went to your house, and you, as you know, weren't there. It's—" He glanced at his watch. "It's two-fifteen if you want to meet me." He hung up without bothering to say good-bye. *She's not coming,* he thought. *No way is she coming. If she was coming, she'd have been at home waiting like she was supposed to be.* He walked over to the closest elevator and jabbed the up button so hard, a jolt of pain went through his finger.

Yeah, Fascinelli, mess up your hand, you moron, he thought. *If you stop being able to throw and catch, you'll be out of that school in one game. And maybe that wouldn't even be so bad. Maybe Jackie was right.*

All right. Enough. This isn't about you, he told himself. *It's about a girl who tried to off herself.* The elevator doors opened, and a couple of tired-looking people stepped off. Anthony got on and gently pressed the button for the fourth floor. When the elevator reached the floor, he made his way to Jackie's room on autopilot, his mind busy replaying all the crap Jackie'd said last time they were together.

Girl. Almost offed self. The rest of it doesn't matter, Anthony thought as he hesitated outside her door. He didn't hear any guest kind of sounds—no talking, no laughing, no crying or little sympathy noises. So it was on him. Anthony pulled in a breath and stepped inside. Jackie was propped up against a bunch of pillows—conscious, at least—but still looking half dead.

"Hey," Anthony said. He knew there should be something better to say. But whatever it was, it wasn't anywhere in his brain.

Jackie smiled, a small trembly-edged smile. *Don't let her start bawling,* Anthony silently begged.

"Hi," she said, meeting his gaze and then quickly glancing away. "I can't believe you're here," she said, talking more to her bedspread than to him.

Anthony sat down in the chair next to her bed. "Yeah, well, I wanted to see how you were."

"Sorry I said all those things to you," Jackie told him, meeting his eyes again. "I didn't really mean them. I was just . . ." Her words trailed off.

"Embarrassed?" Anthony suggested.

"Yeah, mostly," Jackie admitted. "So, um, how's school?"

"It's Saturday," Anthony reminded her. "Not much school happening since . . . you know." He propped his foot on his knee, hoping to get more comfortable. It didn't help. "You want me to get you a soda or candy or something?"

I'm such an idiot, he thought. *I should have brought her something. You always bring someone in the hospital something.*

"No, I'm okay," Jackie told him, switching back to talking down to her blanket.

"Should have brought you something, sorry," Anthony muttered.

"It's fine. Like I need another stuffed animal." Jackie picked up a little stuffed mouse from the nightstand and tossed it at him. "Everyone comes in for a second, hurls an animal or flowers or whatever at me, and then runs. Like I'm contagious. I'd rather have someone to, you know, talk to."

Anthony was hit with the weird sensation that Jackie was like a split personality or something— there was party girl Jackie, who kissed him until he could hardly stand up; bitch Jackie, who made him feel like crawling off and dying in the stairwell; and now . . . Anthony didn't know what to call this Jackie.

"What?" Jackie asked, raising one eyebrow.

"Nothing," he answered. "So, why'd you do it?" he blurted out. He hadn't been planning to say it like that. He thought he'd kind of ease into it somehow. But now—thud—it was out there.

"What is it with you?" Jackie snapped. "Is it some new fetish? You play the big hero guy—'I'll take those car keys, miss, you're in no shape to be driving and might injure yourself'—then go home and jack off?"

Anthony laughed. And it wasn't at all faked. "I'm not leaving until you tell me," he said, making himself more comfortable in the chair. "So, is it a guy?"

"Now I get it," Jackie said. She gave the pillows behind her a fluff. "We kissed one night and you got all squishy inside, and now you're thinking that the only way I couldn't be all gaga over you is that there's another guy somewhere."

"School?" Anthony tossed out. "You been screwing up? Afraid you'll have to go to—" He lowered his voice. "A state college?"

Jackie snorted. *At least she doesn't look half dead anymore,* Anthony thought. Her cheeks were flushed, and her eyes were bright. Because she was pissed off, yeah. But it was still an improvement.

"Stock market?" Anthony suggested. "You having a bad year?"

"What do you know about the stock market?" Jackie asked.

Okay, don't want to go there, Anthony thought. *I don't need the whole you'll-always-be-the-loser-from-Fillmore speech again.* Rae had picked up a little from the stuff in the hospital room. But what? When Rae collapsed, everything else had gone out of his mind.

"Ooh, I'm sorry. Did I touch a nerve?" Jackie asked. "Don't worry about it. I doubt anyone from Fillmore—"

"Phillip," Anthony blurted out, his brain starting to regurgitate what Rae had said. "Is it about Phillip?"

Crap. Oh crap, Anthony thought. Because Jackie's eyes were filling with tears. A second later her shoulders were shaking with silent sobs.

Rae gingerly shifted her position on the motel bed, trying to ease her aching muscles. Whoever had tied her up really knew what they were doing. More than the slightest movement and the ropes—no, they were slicker than that, maybe cords?—binding her tightened.

Stay calm, she told herself. *Stay calm or you won't be ready to—what? Won't be ready to be completely helpless when whoever's holding you prisoner comes back?* Rae's heart started to slam furiously against her rib cage. She tried to pull in a deep breath but couldn't. Her wrist bindings had been tied to her ankle bindings with a short piece of the cord or whatever, so she had to sit hunched over. All she could manage was harsh pants. They came faster and faster until white dots exploded in front of her eyes. *Oh God. I'm blacking out.*

"Rae," Yana called softly.

"Yana, are you in here? Why didn't you answer before?" Rae cried, her voice getting higher with each word.

"Not so loud," Yana warned, her voice low, but with a current of fear running through it that was almost like an electric charge, something that made the hair on Rae's arms stand on end. Yana was never scared.

"But why didn't you answer?" Rae repeated, struggling to keep her voice under control. "Are you okay?"

"Yeah. But I was unconscious. I don't know for how long," Yana answered.

"They *hit* you?" Rae burst out.

"What? Did you think a gang of fluffy bunnies with marshmallow hearts did this to us?" Yana asked. "Anyway, I'm okay. Just got a lump on my head. So did I miss anything while I was out? Give me the soap opera digest."

"One of them tied me up and told me to keep quiet or they'd know. Then the two of them—I think there were just two—left," Rae answered. Talking to Yana had helped her get a little bit of a grip. At least she wasn't hyperventilating anymore.

"So screaming our heads off would probably be a bad idea," Yana said.

"They could be in another state by now, I guess," Rae answered. "But if they aren't—"

"Right," Yana interrupted. "If they aren't and they *are,* like, right next door, and we scream, then they're the ones who come running. And my head isn't ready for round two."

"Eventually someone will miss us. I told my dad I was going out with you, but if I don't make it home tonight, he'll go crazy," Rae said, a salty ball forming in her throat as she thought about her father and how worried he'd be. She swallowed hard. It didn't help much. "But even if he calls the police, they'd never think of looking for us here. Unless—you didn't tell your dad where you were going, did you?"

"I don't tell him anything," Yana answered. Rae could imagine the closed-off expression on her face. "And since there's enough frozen food in the fridge for a couple of days, he probably won't notice I'm gone for, oh, a couple of days."

Rae knew she should say something to make Yana

feel better, but she had no idea what. She'd never even met Yana's father, so she couldn't say that Yana was being too harsh or anything.

The silence stretched out. Thirty seconds. A minute. Suddenly Rae felt like the motel room was expanding, that if she somehow managed to rip off her blindfold, she wouldn't be able to see the walls. She'd be all alone in a scratchy blackness. Even Yana would be too far away to hear her voice.

"Yan?" Rae said, freaked out.

"What?" Yana asked.

"Nothing. I just . . . never mind," Rae answered. "Let's keep talking, okay?"

"Our little trip to the center must have made somebody incredibly nervous," Yana said. "There's definitely something more than knitting going on there. Or at least when your mom was there, there was. We're at the place for fifteen minutes, and the next day we're—"

Rae stiffened, pain shooting through her muscles, as she heard the motel door swing open, then click shut. "Somebody's here," Rae announced, in case Yana was too far away to have heard.

"That's right," a male voice answered. It really didn't sound like Aiden. The voice was deeper—grittier. "Somebody's here. And somebody else better keep quiet and do exactly what they're told." He raised his voice a little. "And you in the bathroom, not one word out of you." It wasn't Aiden—she was almost positive. But the voice *did* sound familiar somehow. Did she know this man from somewhere? Who *was* he?

Rae's hands were untied, quickly, roughly. Something was shoved into her fingers, but she dropped it immediately.

"That's not what I call cooperation," the man said.

"The cord was too tight," Rae protested. "My fingers weren't getting any circulation. Feel them if you don't believe me. They're like ice." Her stomach turned over. She couldn't believe she'd just invited the man to touch her.

"Shake them out," he ordered, and Rae felt something cool and hard press against the back of her head. A gun. He was holding a gun on her.

Rae hurried to obey him, shaking her hands wildly back and forth, feeling like someone was attacking her cold fingers with a staple gun. Slowly warmth and sensation crept back into them, and the man pressed the object into her grip again. This time she was able to keep hold of it—and to recognize it. A cell phone.

"Here's what you're going to do," the man said. "You're going to call your father. You're going to tell him that you and your friend decided to go to a

concert—don't say which one, don't say where—
and that you'll be too tired to drive home tonight, so
you'll see him in the morning."

"But he'll—" Rae began. The gun pressed more
firmly against her head. She could feel the circle of
the metal barrel through her hair.

"That's all you say," the man continued. "I'll
dial." She felt the cell give little jerks as he punched
in the numbers, then he shoved the phone up to her
ear. "No attempts at code or anything like that. I'm
not stupid."

"Hello?" her dad said.

Rae didn't think she could get a word out. The
salty lump had doubled in her throat. She made her
free hand into a fist, digging her nails into her hand,
trying to get enough control of herself to do what she
had to do.

"Hi, it's me." She didn't even attempt to say the
word *dad*. If she did, she'd lose it immediately. "Yana
and I are going to a concert tonight. It's going to end
late, and we're going to be too tired to drive. I'll see
you in the morning."

Immediately the phone was wrenched away. She
hadn't even had the chance to hear her father say one
more word, not even good-bye.

"You two keep being good," the man ordered
as he retied Rae's hands, even more roughly than

before. Rae dug her fingernails deeper into her flesh. She could feel warm blood spreading across her palm, but she didn't let up. She wasn't going to cry, not with him there.

Rae heard the door open, then shut, then lock. Slowly she uncurled her fingers. Her eyes stung, but she managed to hold back the tears. Now wasn't the time, even though she and Yana were alone again.

"He's gone," she said.

"Are you all right?" Yana asked. "All I wanted to do was get free and rip his head off. But the more you try to get these cords off, the tighter they get."

"I know," Rae answered. "Do you think it's weird that he came in just then?"

"Weird how? We thought they were probably nearby," Yana answered.

Rae wiped her bloody palm on the bedspread. "Yeah, but I said that my dad would be worried when I didn't come home tonight, and two minutes later he comes in wanting me to call my dad."

"So you think they're—" Yana began.

"I think they're listening to everything we say," Rae finished for her.

Chapter 12

Jackie wiped her face with the edge of her blanket, taking way more time than necessary. Anthony got that. She needed to get herself back under control. "Can you hand me my purse?" she asked. Anthony spotted a hairy pink thing on a shelf with other stuff that seemed like it belonged to Jackie and tossed it to her.

"I said hand, not throw," she muttered as she started rummaging through it. She pulled out some makeup—lipstick, mascara, something Anthony didn't recognize—then she slid a little mirror out of a plastic sheath and peered at herself.

"God. I look—" She didn't finish, she just got to work, dabbing some makeup under her eyes, then using what looked like a big glue stick to put more makeup on her forehead, down her nose, and across her chin. *She's just going to pretend the whole crying jag didn't happen,* Anthony realized as she started rubbing in the streaks of makeup with her fingers.

The last thing Anthony wanted to do was start her up again, but clearly her brother, Phillip, was a big part of Jackie's problem. All he'd had to do was say the name and—flood. He had to push her. Now. Before she got all armored up again. "So, Phillip," he said.

"What do you know about Phillip?" Jackie asked as she began outlining one of her eyes with a makeup pencil.

"Not much," Anthony admitted. "But he's got a lot to do with your aspirin OD, right?"

"My brother doesn't even live at home," Jackie answered, still working on her face. "Don't you think playing amateur shrink is a little ambitious? Why don't you pretend to be a lifeguard or something?"

Anthony felt a muscle in his jaw twitch and hoped Jackie didn't see it. He didn't want to give her the satisfaction of knowing she was getting to him again.

"I don't exactly need a college education to put it together," Anthony told her. "I say the name Phillip, and you start spewing tears and snot." He grabbed a handful of the sheet she'd been using as Kleenex and waved it in front of her face. Evidence.

"It didn't have anything to do with Phillip," Jackie insisted. "Phillip is the same as he's been for the last five years, the family screwup." Jackie put her finger to her lips and made a loud shushing sound. "But nobody's supposed to know that. Everybody's supposed to think our Phillip is off at boarding school, playing rugby, making the honor roll, and getting ready to make us all proud at the college of his choice."

"So, if he's not there, where is he?" Anthony asked.

Jackie didn't answer for a minute. She'd gotten all busy with her lipstick. Finally she seemed satisfied with the way her mouth looked and answered his question. "Oh, he is in boarding school some of the time. When he's not in rehab." She gave another exaggerated shushing sound. "He got started on Ritalin, then moved on to coke. I think he's still on crystal meth right now. It's hard to know exactly. It's not like anybody bothers to talk to me about it. But I hear things. I do actually live in the house with my parents, whether they realize it or not."

Okay, she wants some attention from Mommy and Daddy. That's what this is all about. He hadn't spent three years listening to Abramson drag crap like this out of people for nothing. What would she say right now?

177

"Have you ever told your parents you want to know what's going on?" Anthony said, doing his Abramson impression. "You know, asked them right out?"

Jackie laughed, a harsh sound that should be called something totally different than a laugh. "You really are stupid, aren't you?" she asked. "Let me spell it out in little words. Phillip is in boarding school. Phillip is wonderful. We are all very, very proud of Phillip. That is all anyone in my family is willing to talk about."

"So when do you get sent to boarding school?" Anthony demanded. "After another cry-for-help aspirin suicide? Or will you have to go for the heavy stuff—razors or whatever?"

"Get out of here," Jackie said, her voice calm and low. She slid her mirror back into its sheath and began replacing her makeup in her purse, not even glancing over to see if he was obeying her command.

He wasn't. He hardly knew the girl. There was no reason for him to give a crap what happened to her. But he did. Maybe because it was so clear she had no one else.

"That's what you want, you know that, right? I mean, you're the smart one here," Anthony told her. "You want your turn to be Phillip. Why should you have to be the one pretending everything is great?

Why shouldn't you get a turn being the screwup?" He figured that's about what Abramson would say. Although she'd have worked it out so that Jackie ended up saying it herself. Anthony didn't have time for that.

Jackie opened her mouth, shut it, then opened it again. She looked like a freakin' fish, but Anthony didn't point that out.

"I don't want to be a screwup," she finally managed to say.

"Chugging vodka and tequila—then driving. Shoplifting," Anthony began.

"I was just having fun," Jackie protested. "I'm still pulling in the grades. I'm still—"

"What was fun about all the aspirin?" Anthony asked.

Jackie did the fish face again.

"You're pissed off at having to keep all the Phillip stuff a secret. You hate pretending everything is fine, right?" Anthony said. He looked at her until she raised her eyes to his.

"Yeah," she admitted.

"Well, that's what you're doing with yourself," he pointed out, pulling another Abramson. "You're trying to pretend that everything is okay with you. In a minute you'll be telling me that you're playing rugby and that you'll have your pick of schools."

Jackie blinked rapidly, and Anthony thought he saw a sheen of tears in her eyes. They didn't spill over, though. Then she smiled, a tiny smile. "My parents would freak if I actually made them talk about Phillip and me and everything. It would be their worst nightmare."

Anthony leaned close to her. "Family counseling," he whispered.

Jackie giggled. "Oh my God. They'd die."

"But if your doctor told them it was necessary . . ." Anthony said.

"I'm sure she would," Jackie agreed. The smile left her face.

Anthony figured it had just hit her that it wouldn't be quite so much fun to actually go through with the counseling. To be in a room with her parents and actually say the things that no one was supposed to say.

"You can do it," Anthony said. "The next time your doctor comes in, talk to her. Or I could talk to her for you."

Jackie shook her head. "No. I can do it myself," she answered. "In fact, why wait for her to come in? My parents are paying enough for this private room and all. Why don't I get her in here right now." She reached out and pushed the call button. "I'll have one of the nurses fetch her for me."

"Should I stay?" Anthony asked.

"No. You're of no more use to me," Jackie answered. But she stretched out her hand and squeezed his arm. She didn't let go until the nurse came into the room.

Anthony stood up and left, turning at the door to give Jackie a wink. *Got through that alive,* he thought as he headed down the hall to the elevators. No thanks to Rae.

He spotted a pay phone and dialed Rae's cell again. No answer. "I just got done here. It went okay, I guess," he said when her voice mail beeped. "I hope you're enjoying yourself wherever you are," he added, then slammed down the phone.

Rae knew she should probably keep quiet. If she and Yana were being monitored, the way they thought they were, then why give the men anything to listen to? But she was pretty sure if she didn't start talking, she'd end up screaming. And then she and Yana would end up dead.

"Yana," she said softly. "Why do you think they had me tell my dad the concert story? It doesn't give them a lot of time. If I don't get home tomorrow, he's still going to go nuts."

"I've been thinking about that, too," Yana answered. Her voice sounded kind of hollow, probably from the acoustics in the bathroom where they'd stuck her. "Maybe they're planning to let us go tomorrow."

Rae wished that was true. But it didn't make sense. "Why would they just keep us overnight?" she asked, hoping Yana had a good reason.

"Maybe they want to know if we found out anything at the center," Yana suggested. "Except they aren't asking us any questions, so . . ." She sighed. "I guess the other thing is they could just be planning to kill us."

The words were like an icicle stabbing into Rae's heart. "Kill?" she managed to repeat.

"The concert thing would be a false lead," Yana explained. "When—if—you don't get home, your dad will call the cops. He'll tell them that you said you were going to a concert. They'd probably check out where there were major concerts around Atlanta last night and see if there were any accidents. If there weren't . . . well, they definitely wouldn't be looking for us in a Motel 6. I don't know. I'm just—" Her voice actually cracked, something Rae had never heard in all the time she'd known her. "I don't know," she finished in a quiet, uncertain tone.

Hearing Yana sound so shaky made the fear in Rae multiply. Yana didn't scare easily. "What time do you think it is?" she asked.

"It feels like it's been days. But maybe it's only been a few hours," Yana said.

By the time I count to a thousand, someone will find us, Rae thought. *Or, no, by the time I count to a million.* When she was a little girl, she'd tried to count to a million a bunch of times, but she always fell asleep, or lost her place, or got distracted. *If I do it this time, Yana and I will be okay.* She knew the thought was ridiculous, at least most of her did. There was a little, teeny piece that still believed in—

Rae jerked, the cords biting into her, as she heard the door swing open and then shut. What was going to happen this time?

The mattress beneath her sank down as someone sat beside her. She could smell something antiseptic. God, she hated that smell. It was a total hospital smell.

Experiments. The word screamed through her mind. Was that why the man had the antiseptic smell? Was he about to do some kind of experiment on her? Maybe the same experiment that had been done on her mother?

Rae heard a rustling sound. And a new odor hit her nose. Tuna fish. A moment later something soft brushed against her lips. Gooseflesh broke out all over her body. He had his hand on her mouth. It was so intimate. The light touch was so much worse than being roughly tied up.

"Eat," the man ordered.

It's not his fingers, Rae realized. *It's bread. It's a tuna sandwich.* The bread was pushed more firmly against her lips. "I'm not hungry," she said. But her stomach growled, and saliva flooded her mouth. "I'm not hungry," she repeated. She wasn't going to eat anything they gave her. It could be drugged. It could be poisoned. It could be—

"Eat," the man said again. And then his hands were on her mouth, his fingers prying open her lips and teeth. He shoved the sandwich at her again, and Rae choked down a bite. The man jammed the sandwich at her lips again before she'd even finished swallowing. Rae took another bite, wanting to get this over with, wanting him to get away from her. She started to choke, flecks of the sandwich flying out of her mouth.

"Drink this," the man instructed. Rae felt hard plastic against her lips. The man put one hand on her forehead and pressed until she tilted her head back a little. Then she felt water streaming into her mouth and down her chin. She swallowed convulsively, managing to get some down.

"Do you need to use the bathroom?" the man asked Rae when he'd finished feeding her. She wanted to say no, but the pressure on her bladder had gone from annoying to painful. Was he going to watch her pee? She had to say no. But how many more hours would they be kept here? God, what if she ended up peeing all over herself. Would he clean her up or— "Yes or no," the man prompted.

"Yeah," Rae answered. Her chest was pulled closer to her knees as the man grabbed the rope connecting her hands and feet. The breath was squeezed out of her lungs, and she felt like her rib cage was compressing, pressing against her heart. Then, abruptly, the pressure was gone. Rae was able to straighten her spine for the first time in . . . however long she'd been sitting on the bed in the Motel 6. Each vertebra burned as she gently twisted from side to side, but it still felt so good to get out of that hunched-over position.

"On your feet," the man said. He didn't wait for her to respond, just grabbed her by the elbow and pulled her up, then led her out into the hall, Rae stumbling with the tiny baby steps that were all the cords would allow her.

Where is everyone in this place? she thought. *Why isn't anyone here to see me get dragged blindfolded through the hall?* And why was the man even risking it? Why didn't he make her use the bathroom where Yana was?

Rae heard a knock on a door and then a door opening, and she was pulled into what she figured was another motel room. After a few more stumbling steps she heard another door open, and then there was tile under her feet instead of carpet. The man untied her hands and guided them to cool porcelain. "This is the toilet. You have thirty seconds. Don't take off the blindfold."

That voice . . . she *knew* she recognized it. If she could just remember where she'd heard it before. But her brain couldn't seem to make the connection.

Footsteps moved across the tile, then Rae heard the door close. *Thirty seconds,* she thought, jerking herself into action. She got her pants and underpants down—no farther than they had to go—and felt for the toilet seat and sat, trying to keep her thighs apart even though her feet were tied together. Then nothing. Her bladder was aching, but nothing. *They're not watching,* Rae told herself. But she knew they were there—at least two of them—right on the other side of the door. With guns. Waiting to tie her back up. Waiting to—

Rae stretched out her hands to both sides. She fumbled around until she found the sink and then turned on the water. It worked. She was able to pee. The second she was through, she struggled to her feet and yanked her panties up. She was zipping up her pants when she heard the door open.

The man—same one, different one?—tied her hands again. Rae winced as the cords tightened over a raw spot on the inside of her left wrist. "Okay, move," the man said. It was the same guy as before—that familiar voice. Every time he spoke she seemed to get closer and closer to placing it, but the answer still wouldn't come. She knew it wasn't Aiden, and she was starting to feel certain that Aiden actually hadn't been involved in this at all. The woman who'd called her had said she was calling for Aiden, but she must have been lying. She'd known somehow about Rae visiting the center and meeting Aiden, and she'd used that to lure Rae here. So whoever kidnapped her had done it because she was at the Wilton Center, getting too close to something. But she'd been right about her sense that Aiden wasn't a threat—he was terrified himself, probably terrified of these very people.

"I said, move." The man jerked her up by her arm and marched her back into the other room, where he sat her down on the bed. Rae was hoping he'd leave off the cord between her hands and feet, but he didn't. A little cry of pain escaped her as her back was pulled into the bent-over position again.

"Now you're going to make one more phone call,"

the man told her. "Should have done it before I got you tied back up. Tell me the number of your boyfriend."

"What?" Rae asked, and the man cuffed the side of her head.

"Anthony. He's been leaving messages for you. You're going to tell him the same thing you told your dad. Nothing else. Now, what's his number?" the man asked.

Suddenly it hit her—with a force so strong she couldn't believe it had taken her this long. The man's voice was giving her that same creepy chill in her spine that she'd felt very recently. It was the sensation she'd gotten standing in front of her house talking to the meter reader who wasn't really a meter reader.

Oh my god, she realized, her heart racing. It was the same man—one of her kidnappers had already been that close to her, talking to her in broad daylight. Was there something she could have done before now?

"Are you looking to get hurt here?" the man asked, a strong edge to his tone. "What is the number? *Now.*"

Rae swallowed, trying to slow her pulse, then recited the number in as calm a tone as possible. She heard the little beeps as the man punched it in, then she felt the cell phone against her ear. *This could be your only chance,* she thought. *You've got to find a way to—*

"Hello?"

"Anthony? Hi, sweetie, it's me." *That should give him a clue right there,* Rae thought. Hoped. "Yana and I decided to go to a concert tonight."

"What the hell—" Anthony began.

Rae kept talking. She didn't have much time. "Sorry I didn't tell you. We're going to be wiped, so we'll crash before we come back. It's like that time Yana and I went to New Orleans—an impulse thing. But closer to home."

The man pulled the phone away from her ear. *Did Anthony get it?* Rae wondered. Had she made it clear enough?

I should have known something was wrong, Anthony thought. He ate one of his curly fries, and his stomach rolled over. Anthony pushed the plate away. *I just assumed she blew me off to hang with Yana, but I should have known it was something else. She's the one who said we should go back and see Jackie again. It was her idea. I'm such a freakin' idiot.*

He caught a flash of movement out of the corner of his eye and looked up to see Jesse rushing across the Chick-fil-A toward him. "So what happened?" Jesse asked as he slid into the seat across from Anthony.

"I don't know anything more than what I told you on the phone," Anthony answered. "Have you talked to Rae at group? Do you know if she's—"

"She hasn't told me anything," Jesse interrupted. "Don't you guys see each other at school all the time?"

"Not really. We don't have classes or anything together," Anthony answered.

"But if there was some big thing, she'd tell you," Jesse insisted.

Would she? Things had been screwed up between them since he started at her school. They were starting to get okay again when they went to see Jackie together, but—

"Well?" Jesse pressed, grabbing a few of Anthony's fries.

"Eat them all," Anthony told him. Just the smell was making him want to spew. "I think we should just focus on what she said when she called me. She was trying to tell me something, but whatever it is, I didn't get it."

"Okay, tell me what she said again," Jesse answered. He tore open a little packet of ketchup and squirted it on the fries. *Like blood,* Anthony thought, his mouth getting all wet with that pre-puking feeling. He forced his gaze to Jesse's face.

"She said that she and Yana were going to a concert and that they'd be tired, so they were crashing before they came home. And then she said it was like the time she and Yana had gone to New Orleans—an impulse thing. But closer to home," Anthony answered. "She called me sweetie, too, but I think that was just to let me know something was wrong. I don't think it was part of whatever she was trying to tell me about where she and Yana are."

Jesse added more ketchup to the curly fries and started scarfing them. Anthony took a long swallow of his Sprite, hoping it would keep his stomach under control. "Okay, so concert. Have you and Rae ever been to one? Or has she talked about one she wanted to see or anything?"

"Rae and I haven't really been talking much lately," Anthony admitted. Jesse shot him a questioning look, but Anthony didn't say any more. He didn't want to talk about the weirdness that had been going on between him and Rae. He didn't want to think about it. All he wanted was to get her back.

"She can't have been trying to tell me she was in New Orleans," Anthony said. "Otherwise she wouldn't have said the closer-to-home part." Crap. If he was smarter, he'd already know where she was. What was—

"Okay, so closer to home. Does that mean Atlanta, you think? Like near her house? Or someplace near Atlanta?" Jesse asked, chain eating the last few fries. "Maybe we should check out what bands are playing. Maybe one of the band names will mean something." Jesse leaned over to the empty table across from them and grabbed the newspaper lying there.

Would Rae even know what bands were playing where? Anthony realized he didn't have a clue. There was so much he didn't know about her. He'd spent all this time around her and—

"Okay, we got the Blake Babies at the Echo Lounge. Slash's Snakepit at the Roxy. And Propagandhi, Fabulous Disaster, and J Church at the different Masquerade levels," Jesse said. "Those are the big places. Mean anything to you?"

"Nothing." Anthony scrubbed his forehead. He felt like tumors as big and hard as marbles were sprouting all over in his brain. He was never smart, but now— "She could die because I can't understand what she was trying to tell me."

"Slash's Snakepit, Blake Babies, J Church, Fabulous Disaster, Propagandhi," Jesse muttered. "Roxy, Echo, Masquerade." He took his finger and ran it across the ketchup-smeared plate, then licked the ketchup off his finger. "Doesn't mean anything to me, either." He moved his finger toward the plate again. Anthony snatched up the paper plate and crumpled it. Jesse raised his eyebrows but didn't say anything.

"Sorry," Anthony muttered. "Just—sorry." He shoved his fingers into his hair and rubbed the top of his head. It didn't help. "The New Orleans part seems the most important. But the hell if I know what she meant." Anthony wanted to slam their table down to the floor or shove his fist into the face of one of the people happily chowing down. He wanted to do anything. Anything but sit here while Rae was . . . while Rae was who knew where having who knew what done to her.

"You guys went to New Orleans to talk to my dad," Jesse reminded him.

"Yeah. Before you got here, I was thinking about that trip," Anthony answered. "Thinking about it until my head felt like it would explode. But nothing. We drove in. Got fake IDs. Went to this club called Hurricanes, where your dad was bartending. And that's it. Except we spent the night at the—" Anthony closed his eyes and groaned. "I am such a moron. That's it. We spent the night at a Motel 6. There are at least three of them in Atlanta. That could be what she meant when she said they were crashing and that it was like the time in New Orleans."

"So we need a phone book, then we're on our way," Jesse said.

Anthony was already on his feet.

Chapter 13

Rae felt like she was floating in blackness, as if her whole world was the soft blackness of her blindfold.

"I feel like I'm about an inch above my body," Yana said.

"Huh?" As soon as the word was out of her mouth, Rae realized she'd actually heard what Yana'd said. There'd just been this weird time delay between hearing and understanding. "Me too," she answered. "Like I'm hovering right above myself."

"Do you think they're listening?" Yana asked. "Do you think we were right?"

"Maybe," Rae said. It didn't seem to matter much if they were right or wrong. Nothing seemed to matter much. "Have you ever fallen asleep with your eyes open?" Rae answered her own question before Yana had the chance. "I did once, at a slumber party. We were trying to stay up all night, and I didn't want to be the first one to go to sleep. But I did somehow, without even closing my eyes. When I woke up—I think it was only maybe a minute later—everyone was staring at me like I was some kind of freak."

"Nuh-uh. Never happened to me," Yana answered. "But I never went to many slumber parties."

Rae always forgot how different their lives had been . . . how different they still were, even though they were friends. *And if it weren't for me, Yana wouldn't be here,* Rae thought with a fresh stab of guilt. Yet another person she cared about that she'd managed to drag into danger.

"Are you scared?" Rae asked. "I know I should be scared—terrified—but I just feel all—"

"Floaty," Yana finished for her.

"Yeah," Rae agreed.

"I feel like I could just float through the ceiling. Except I really have to pee," Yana said.

"Again?" Rae still felt too separate from her body for hunger or thirst or having to pee.

"What do you mean, again? I haven't been able to go since they grabbed us. The cords are too tight for me to even stand up," Yana told her.

"Did they give you food?" Rae asked.

"You got food?" Yana replied.

Rae frowned, and the movement reconnected her to her body. Every bone felt jagged. Her muscles were like sandpaper. Every place where the cords touched her skin burned and itched.

"I don't get it. Why'd they let me eat and—" Rae began. The answer came like a hammer blow to the head. "It's because they only care about me," she said. "There's something they want from me. You just happened—"

Rae stopped herself before she finished speaking the thought aloud. But she couldn't keep the truth from herself. The men didn't care about Yana. They wouldn't care if Yana died right now.

"God, Yana, I'm sorry," Rae burst out. "If I didn't get you to come with me—"

"Oh, shut up," Yana snapped. "It's not like you knew this was going to happen."

"Everybody I let get close to me gets hurt," Rae insisted, thinking of Anthony, thinking of Jesse.

"Oh, poor you," Yana said. "Instead of wasting time feeling sorry for yourself, you should be helping me come up with some kind of plan."

"Except that we're pretty sure they're listening," Rae reminded Yana. She tilted her head from side to side, trying to crack her neck. "What time do you think it is? Could it be morning already? Do you think my dad will already be looking for me to be back from the concert?"

Saying the word *dad* killed the rest of the floaty feeling. Rae shuddered, the cords digging tighter, as the reality of the situation slammed into her, the fear as fresh as when the man grabbed her and blindfolded her and—

"My dad . . ." Yana began.

"What?" Rae asked when Yana didn't continue.

"I was just trying to remember the last time I actually believed my dad gave a crap about me," Yana said slowly. "I think I was about seven. Yeah, the first half of my seventh birthday. By the end, I knew he couldn't care less."

"Why? What happened?" Rae asked.

"Forget it. Doesn't matter," Yana muttered.

"I'll tell you something if you tell me," Rae bargained. There was no response from Yana. "Okay, something about me. I used to be a total dork back when I was Rachel."

Yana snorted. "You're still Rachel."

"Oh, no, no, no. I'm Rae."

"Big difference," Yana commented.

"Huge. Rachel, when she was in the sixth grade, I'm talking the *sixth* grade, used to pretend she was an alien from the planet Gloopus, an alien named Princess Tamasela."

"Catchy," Yana said.

"Dorky," Rae corrected. "Mockage worthy." She could almost see herself hopping around the baseball field of her school, pretending to be on one of the giant kangaroos that populated Gloopus. "So seventh birthday," she prompted Yana.

"Seventh birthday," Yana repeated. She sighed, loudly enough for Rae to hear from the next room. "Okay. Possibly hard to believe, but I was the ultimate girlie girl when I was a kid." She paused a second. Two. Ten.

"What, no tattoos?" Rae gently teased, trying to get Yana going again.

"No way. Ballerinas didn't have tattoos, and that's what I wanted to be—a ballerina. For my birthday my dad got a pair of tickets to the local ballet company—we were living in Buffalo back then. I was ecstatic. I picked out what I was going to wear two weeks in advance. I picked out what my dad was going to wear."

Yana spoke faster and faster, like someone had pulled out a stopper inside her. "I practiced putting my hair in one of those really tight, slicked-back ballerina buns. I mean so tight, it would give me a headache. And I went to the school library and read about the history of the ballet so I'd have interesting stuff to tell my dad at intermission."

She sucked in a breath and rushed on. "So my birthday gets there. Finally. And my dad's late getting home. No big deal. Except that it gets later and later, and he still doesn't show. He doesn't get home by the time the ballet starts. He doesn't get home by the time the ballet ends. He gets home at two-sixteen in the morning. And he yells at me for still being awake."

"God," Rae murmured. She could see little Yana as clearly as she'd pictured little Rachel. She imagined Yana with one of those rings of little plastic flowers around her bun. She saw Yana's hair as light brown back then before Yana got into bleaching it. "Did he just forget?" Rae asked.

"Didn't ask," Yana answered, her voice tightening again, returning to the usual brisk tone.

"I'm taking you to the ballet when we get out of here," Rae promised, hurting with the desire to do something for her friend.

"Can you see me at the ballet now? I don't think so," Yana told Rae.

"It'd be fun," Rae said.

"Just forget about it, okay?" Yana's voice was harsh now, like she was mad at Rae. "I don't know why I told you in the first place."

"I'm glad you told me." Rae hesitated, then decided to tell the truth. It was stupid not to when they might not ever get out of this room alive. "I know we haven't been friends for that long, but you're my best friend, Yana. That probably sounds dorky, like I'm still that dorky Rachel girl. Who actually says 'best friend' past elementary school? But it's true. You are my best friend. And what you told me, that's exactly the kind of stuff best friends tell each other."

Yana was silent for a moment. "You're my best friend, too, Rae," Yana finally answered. She sounded so strangely serious about it.

"I wish you weren't in here with me," Rae told her. "But I'm really glad you are, you know?"

She pulled in a deep breath. There was a big secret she'd been keeping from Yana. Huge. Anthony knew. And Jesse. But Rae'd wanted one person in her life who just thought of her as normal.

You should tell her, Rae thought. But what if it made Yana sick? What if it made her think Rae was a total freak? What if she started treating Rae like one of the really delusional patients in the hospital?

What if, what if, what if. What if they never made it out of this motel alive? At least she would have come clean with the one person left she could totally trust. And even if someone *was* listening to them, she and Anthony had already figured out that whoever was after her knew what she could do. *You've got to tell her sometime,* she told herself. *How can you really call her your best friend if you don't?*

"Pizza delivery," Anthony called loudly. He gave two loud knocks on the motel-room door, resisting the urge to put his fist through the freakin' thing. This was the last room to check. If Rae wasn't there, she wasn't anywhere in the place. "Pizza delivery," Anthony called again.

There was no reply. He didn't hear anyone moving around in there, not one tiny sound. "Where is the next Motel 6?" he asked Jesse.

"On Sherman. The one near the car dealership," Jesse said.

Anthony threw the empty pizza box on the floor. Jesse picked it up. "We might need it. There might not be one in the Dumpster at the next place."

What if she's not at the next place? Anthony wondered as he led the way down the stairs to the parking lot. *What if I was too big an idiot to figure out what she was really telling me on the phone?*

"Anthony," Jesse said loudly. "You just passed the car."

Great. He'd walked right by the Hyundai, for chrissake. And he was supposed to be finding Rae? Anthony pulled in a deep breath, turned around, and strode back over to the car. He got in and forced himself to close the door without slamming the hell out of it. He had to get in game head. Get calm. Get focused. For Rae.

"Put on your seat belt," he told Jesse. Then Anthony pulled out of the parking lot and onto the street. He wanted to floor it, but that wasn't smart. If he got pulled over, it would take time, and he didn't have any time to spare. He wasn't sure he even had any time left.

It took about twenty minutes to get to the Sherman Avenue Motel 6. Longest twenty minutes of Anthony's life. He swung the car into the parking lot and felt like he'd been struck by lightning. "That's Yana's car!"

"At least this time we're sure that they're inside," Jesse said.

"Yeah," Anthony answered. "But how do we get them out?"

I'm so close now. I can feel it. Soon I will know everything about Rae, including who else is so interested in her. And then she will die. And I will be the one to kill her.

I can almost hear her screams now. I can almost see her blood. I can almost feel her last breath leaving her body. Soon I'll be able to make it happen. Nothing will stop me. No one can stop me. I will not allow anyone to take the revenge that belongs to me. Rae is mine.

* * *

What was Yana thinking? What was she going to say? Did she think Rae was a disgusting freak? Rae twisted her hands together, even though it made the cords feel like they were sawing their way down to her wrist bones.

"It's almost impossible to believe," Yana finally said. "But I believe you," she added quickly.

That doesn't tell me anything, Rae wanted to scream. Even Yana's voice hadn't given a hint of how Yana was feeling. It had been flat, neutral. Sort of like a nurse talking to a ranting patient.

"You don't really believe me, do you? You think I'm getting sick again," Rae demanded. Her own voice was full of emotion—quivering, making it clear she was about to cry. God, why couldn't she have asked the question in the same tone Yana had used?

"If I could reach you, I would smack you on the head," Yana answered. This time Rae could hear irritation in Yana's voice, and it made Rae smile. Yana wasn't treating her like some poor sick girl. "I said I believe you, and I believe you," Yana continued. "It's just . . ."

"Overwhelming," Rae finished for her.

"Yeah, I feel like my head's been injected with novocaine or something. No wonder you ended up in the hospital. I'd probably still be in there if I were you."

Rae didn't hear any disgust buried in Yana's tone. Or any fear. *I could have told her a long time ago,* she realized. But she hadn't been sure. She didn't want to lose the one girlfriend she had left. The one person she could hang out with and feel actually normal.

"Does your dad know?" Yana asked.

"No. He wouldn't—he'd put me back in the hospital. He'd think he was doing it for my own good," Rae answered.

"But you could prove it to him, right? You could prove it to anybody," Yana said.

"I guess. I never actually thought about it like that. It's weird, huh?" Rae answered. "I still think my dad would want me in the hospital or someplace even if I did make him believe. He'd probably want tests and stuff to be sure that I'm okay, and then everybody would know. I'd be this *abnormality* for life."

"So that's your biggest secret, huh?" Yana asked.

Rae laughed, relief spiraling through her body. "You already know about Gloopus, so, yep, that's it. I'm a fingerprint reader." Telling Yana had been the right thing to do. Rae felt like she'd just dropped a bag full of bowling balls, a bag she'd been carrying around for a long time.

"I think that's why we're in here," Rae continued.

"At least part of the reason. Whoever did this knows about my . . . my *ability*. They found out when they kidnapped Jesse." She thought about adding that she'd recognized one of their kidnapper's voices as that fake meter reader guy, but didn't—just in case he really was listening. She knew their chances of getting out of here were small, but somehow she had a feeling that letting the man know she could ID him would be a bad move either way.

"Maybe they want to use you for, I don't know, terrorist missions or something," Yana suggested. "Like in that show *La Femme Nikita.*"

"Never saw it. TV is a tool of Satan in my house, remember?" Rae answered. "But why keep us here if that's what they wanted? I don't get it. What are they waiting for?"

Not that Rae wanted them to do anything. But eventually they would, and she'd rather know what they had planned.

"Do you smell something?" Yana asked.

Rae pulled in a deep breath. Her heart began to race. She pulled in another breath just to be sure. "Smoke," she told Yana. "I . . . I think the motel is on fire."

She wrenched herself to her feet, the cord tying her hands to her feet keeping her head low. Was there a window in this place? She had to find it. She and Yana weren't going to die in here.

Rae managed a step, then another. She kept expecting to hear the door slam open, but it didn't. She took another tiny step, teetered, then felt herself start to fall. And with her hands tied, unable to block her fall, she hit the ground with a sickening thud, her forehead slamming against something hard.

The fire alarm started to ring. *Hope no one figures out too fast that the fire is just in the Dumpster,* Anthony thought.

Almost immediately a few doors on the bottom level of the Motel 6 opened. Anthony scanned the people coming out, most of them pulling on clothes as they went. No Rae. No Yana. *But they're here,* he told himself.

"You stay by their car," Anthony ordered Jesse. "I'm checking inside." He couldn't stand still. He bolted for the outside staircase, pushing his way against the tide of people all trying to get away from the motel. He took the stairs three at a time, then burst through the entrance into the second-floor hallway.

Except for the alarm bells, it was silent. No doors slamming. No people yelling. No people anywhere. The whole floor couldn't be empty, could it? "Fire!" Anthony shouted. He crisscrossed his way down the hall, pounding on doors. "Fire! Fire! Fire!" Nothing. No response.

Anthony turned and started back down the hall toward the exit. Then he heard something underneath the fire alarms, something that stopped him dead. Someone was—not yelling, exactly, but *trying* to yell. He followed the horrible sound to room 212.

"Rae, are you in there?" The sound grew louder, more frantic. "It's Anthony. I'm here." He tried the doorknob. Locked, of course. Then he took a few steps back, turned his shoulder to the door, and hurled himself at it. He felt something give, but it would take a bunch more solid hits to break the door down. And who knew what was happening to Rae in there. "Hold on, okay? Hold on!" he shouted.

He charged to the exit and out to the staircase. "Jesse," he yelled down to the parking lot. "I found them. Room 212. Get a maid or something. We need the key."

Jesse'd started running toward the motel office before Anthony finished telling him what to do. Anthony raced back to room 212 and put both hands on the door. "A couple of seconds more," he yelled. "I'm right here."

He pressed his hands harder against the door, wanting to slam them through and snatch Rae out of there. "Come on, come on, come on," he muttered. As if in answer, he heard footsteps pounding toward him. He snapped his head toward them. Jesse.

"Master key. Couldn't find anyone, so I took it." Jesse thrust it into Anthony's hand. Anthony missed the lock completely the first time. Cursing himself, he forced himself to slow down, and he finally got the door open.

The first thing he saw was Rae. His eyes went right to her. She was lying on the floor, bound and blindfolded. "Her friend should be here, too. Check the bathroom," he told Jesse.

With two long strides he was next to Rae. He dropped to his knees and pulled the blindfold off. Her blue eyes looking up at him were the most beautiful things he'd ever seen. "Who did this to you?" he demanded. "Doesn't matter," he answered before she could. "Are you okay?" He gently touched her forehead. "You're bleeding."

"I'm fine. Just get me out of here," Rae answered.

"Jesse, you got your knife?" Anthony called.

"One second," Jesse answered. "I'm just getting the last of this girl's cords. Okay, heads up." Jesse leaned out of the bathroom and hurled the pocketknife at Anthony.

Anthony caught it, then flipped it open. With one cut he severed the cord between her hands and her feet. The cords around her ankles and wrists were harder. Rae had her bottom lip locked between her teeth, and he could tell he was hurting her. "Almost done, almost done," he murmured. And she was free.

He locked his arm around her waist and helped her to her feet. Jesse was already helping Yana out the door. "They—whoever did this—they were in the room across the hall," Rae told him.

"The bastards must have run," Anthony told her. He pulled her closer to him, trying to take as much of her weight as he could as they rushed from the room. She gave a little mew of pain as they started down the hall.

The sound was like a knife to the gut. Anthony scooped Rae up in his arms. She pressed herself against his chest, her arms around his neck. He thought he felt blood from her forehead seeping through his shirt. If they were here, if those guys were still here—Anthony shoved the thought away. He needed to focus on Rae right now. She was all that mattered. He slowed down when he hit the stair-case, not wanting to hurt her any more than she'd already been hurt. As soon as his feet reached the asphalt of the parking lot, he began to run again. He didn't stop until he reached his car.

Slowly, carefully, he lowered Rae to her feet. He kept his arms around her. He couldn't let her go.

Nothing could have pulled him away from her, and her arms stayed tight around his neck.

"You found me," she murmured. Her face was so close to his that he could feel her warm breath against his lips.

"What? You thought I wouldn't?" Anthony asked, the question coming out in a choked whisper.

"You found me," she repeated. She tightened her arms around his neck, pulling him so close that their noses touched. His eyes were looking directly into hers, the glistening, vibrant blue filling his vision.

Rae's eyes dropped down, and Anthony knew she was looking at his lips. They started to burn. It was like she was touching them, rubbing them with her fingers.

Then his lips were on hers. Hungry. Urgent. Anthony didn't know how it happened. He didn't care. God, it was Rae. He was kissing Rae. She was alive. He slid one hand up her back and deep into her hair. It was softer than he'd imagined it, even. He was never letting go. Never.

But he wanted to get even closer. Had to. He slid his free hand under her shirt, desperate to feel her skin. *Rae. It's Rae,* he thought. *Rae.*

He never wanted to let go of the warmth of her body. He never wanted to be separated from the wet, warm sweetness of her mouth.

"Anthony, come on. We've got to get out of here," he heard Jesse say from far, far away.

He knew Jesse was right. He knew they were still in danger. But he knew something else—he knew if he pulled away now, it would rip his heart out of his chest. In fact, he wasn't sure if he could ever pull away again.

turn the page
for a preview of
fingerprints #5:

betrayed

Chapter 1

Rae Voight closed her eyes. She felt her body sink down into her soft bed. Deeper, deeper, her breath becoming deeper, too. Slower. Then her right leg kicked out. Her head jerked back. And her eyes snapped open. "You're not there anymore," she whispered, hoping that saying the words out loud would help her believe them. "You're home. You're safe."

Safe. But for how long? The men who had held her and Yana captive in the Motel 6 hadn't found out whatever it was they wanted to know. Whoever they were, they weren't finished with her. Rae didn't think they'd be finished until she was dead. Or they were.

Rae's eyes began to itch. She needed to blink, but

she didn't want to shut her eyes again, even for a fraction of a second. If she did, it would happen. She'd be back in the Motel 6, tied up, helpless. The itching increased. Rae had to blink. Had to. She flicked her eyelids down—and saw herself on the floor of the motel room. She could actually feel the thick, nubby blindfold pressing against her eyes, even though her eyelids had already flicked back up.

Light. She needed light. Rae sat up in bed and switched on the lamp on her nightstand. There was no way she was ever getting to sleep, not when closing her eyes long enough to blink freaked her out. She glanced at her alarm clock—a little after 4 A.M. Thank God. She could get up in another hour or so without her dad going into parental concern overdrive. Rae blinked as fast as she could. Having the light on definitely helped somehow, even during a blink.

A plan. I need some kind of plan, she thought. But her brain was blank, like a fried computer. *Okay, so I'll get Yana and Anthony to help. Maybe even Jesse. I'll ask them all to meet up here after—*

Rae's heart went still, then gave a hard double thump. Someone was in the hall. They were trying to be quiet, but she knew they were there. What if it was him—her kidnapper? The non–meter reader. The man she'd been so close to without knowing what he was capable of, what he would soon do to her. She

2

heard the whisper of cloth—a sleeve? a pant leg?—against the wall. And there—just then—the soft creak of a floorboard. Rae knew that board. It was the loose one about three steps from her bedroom door. Whoever was out there was close. Very close. She jerked her eyes to the window. Closed. Locked. There wouldn't be time to—

A faint squeak interrupted her thoughts. Rae whipped her head back toward the door, her eyes riveted on the doorknob, the turning doorknob. She opened her mouth to scream—and her father stepped into the room.

"Dad," Rae exclaimed, the word coming out cracked from her dry throat.

"I saw your light. I was up to use the bathroom," he said, jamming his hands in the deep pockets of his worn terry cloth robe.

"I was, um, studying. History test tomorrow," Rae explained, realizing a moment too late that she had no book out, no notebook, nothing.

"Actually, I was lying," her father told her. "I couldn't sleep."

"Me either," Rae admitted. She scooted closer to the headboard so she could lean against it.

Her father sat down on the edge of the bed. "I kept replaying all the things I said to you when you got home from the concert. I was too harsh. I—"

"No. You were right. It was completely wrong of me to just call and announce I was crashing after the concert and wouldn't be home until morning." Rae didn't tell him she'd been forced by her kidnappers to tell him that lie. If her dad knew what really happened Saturday night, he'd never let her out of his sight again. And he'd probably give himself an ulcer. She remembered how he'd looked when he used to come visit her in the hospital after her breakdown. He'd looked like he should be in the hospital himself, his skin all gray, his clothes loose from the weight he'd lost. Rae never wanted to see him like that again. Especially not because of her.

"Ever since . . . summer," her father began. Rae knew he really meant ever since she'd been put in the mental hospital. "Ever since then, I know I've been a pain." A burst of laughter escaped Rae. That was so not what she was expecting her dad to say. "Buying you that cell phone so I could always check up on you," he continued. "And remember how I wanted to get a live-in housekeeper?" he asked.

"Yeah. I remember," Rae told him. It had taken her at least a week to talk him out of that one.

"I want you to know that it's not that I don't trust you. You have more sense than most of my college students," her dad said. He rubbed the bump on his nose, the bump that Rae had inherited. "It's just that

4

even when you're my age, I'm probably going to feel like it's my job to keep you safe. Last summer—no, last spring, last fall, or even before that, I should have seen—"

"No," Rae cut him off. "It—it wasn't like that. It happened really fast. There was nothing for you to see." That was the truth. Rae's fingerprint-reading power had appeared like a light switch being turned on. At first she'd thought she was going nuts, that she was hearing voices in her head like a psycho killer. Then she'd realized—well, Anthony Fascinelli had realized—what was really going on. When Rae touched a fingerprint, she got the thought the person who left the print was having. "And I'm okay now. I really am," she added.

"I guess we should both get a little sleep," her father answered. He clicked off her lamp. "Next time you want to stay over somewhere after a concert or something, ask first. I'll probably manage to give permission for you to be out of my sight for that long."

"I will," Rae said as he headed out. He shut the door behind him, returning the room to full darkness. Rae realized she'd been blinking away during their whole conversation with no trauma flashes.

So I just need to keep myself distracted, she thought. There was only one thing she could think of that had the power to occupy every molecule of her brain now that she was alone in the dark again—that kiss. That body-melting kiss between her and Anthony after he found her at the motel, found her and carried her to safety.

Experimentally Rae closed her eyes, trying to remember every detail. One of his hands had been twined in her hair, his fingers grazing the back of her neck. That one touch had been enough to send lava down her body. But Anthony'd had one hand under her shirt, on her bare back. And his lips, his tongue . . . God. She'd never felt anything like it. Never. It was like she'd walked around her whole life with her body set on six and Anthony had cranked it up to ten. Heat began pumping through Rae again just thinking about it.

I'm never falling asleep now, she thought. But she didn't care. This was worth staying awake for. Rae replayed the kiss over and over, and it only gained in intensity. When her clock radio began to play, she could hardly believe that hours had passed. Had she actually fallen asleep? If she had, a dream had started exactly where her imagination had left off. She'd spent every moment with Anthony, awake or asleep. She was certain of that.

What am I going to wear? The thought had her out of bed and on her feet in seconds. She rushed over to the closet, yanked it open, and studied the contents. *Like*

Anthony actually notices what you wear, she thought.

Except that he probably did, in that guy way. Maybe he wouldn't be able to say what she'd had on a minute after she was out of his sight, but he'd have an impression—sexy or girlie or something.

Rae ran her finger along the row of clothes. She stopped on her suede skirt, the short one. Anthony liked to look at her in that. She'd seen it on his face. Maybe he couldn't say the color or what it was made of, but it was one of his favorites. Rae picked out a light blue cashmere sweater set to go with it and a pair of flats. She didn't mind it when her heels made her taller than Anthony was, but she was pretty sure he hated it.

After she carefully laid out her clothes on the bed, ignoring the soft buzz of her own old thoughts, Rae hurried to the bathroom. She wanted time to do the hair mud pack and give her legs a quick shave so she could wear the skirt.

Rae only stepped out of the shower when the water turned cold. She knew her father would give her grief for hogging the hot water—he was always saying it should be absolutely impossible for the two of them to come close to using all the water in the reservoir of the hot-water heater. But Rae didn't care. In a little more than an hour, she'd be seeing Anthony. Yeah, it was true that she saw him all the time. But that kiss— that kiss had changed everything. It had for her, at least. And from the way he'd acted as he drove her home early Sunday morning after dropping off Jesse and Yana—so quiet and serious—she was pretty sure Anthony felt the same way.

What am I going to say to him? she wondered as she started to dry her hair. *Do I mention the kiss—no. That would be lame. But am I supposed to just act like nothing is different? Just say hi—and oh, yeah, thanks for saving my life—then head off to my locker?*

What am I going to say to him? Rae was still wondering as she headed toward the main entrance of Sanderson Prep an hour later. She scanned the crowd, and her heart slammed against her ribs as she spotted Anthony leaning against the railing of the front steps. For an instant she felt like she was in his arms again, being carried out of the motel. She could actually feel the heat of his body.

Was that fake meter reader kidnapper watching me and Anthony in the motel parking lot Saturday night? she thought. *Is he already making a new plan to get whatever it is he wants from me?*

And then kill me, she couldn't stop herself from adding.

You're coming up with a plan, too, she reminded herself. *You and Anthony, and Yana and Jesse.* She took one step toward Anthony, then someone grabbed her by the elbow. Rae jerked away.

"Sorry. Did I scare you?" Marcus Salkow asked.

Rae let out a short breath. "A little. I didn't see you come up," she said. And she wished he hadn't. She wanted to get over to Anthony. Right now.

Marcus shifted awkwardly from foot to foot, which was so not the usual Marcus Salkow, school demigod. *Is he going to ask me out again?* Rae wondered. *Is he going to try and convince me to take him back right here and now?*

"I got this for you." Marcus pulled a long velvet box out of his football jacket and thrust it at her. "It's to say I'm sorry—for what a jerk I was when you were in the hospital. I know it really hurt you. Me getting together with Dori without telling you and everything."

"You didn't have to." Rae didn't open the box. "You already apologized, and—"

"It's not just for that," Marcus interrupted. He clicked his teeth together nervously. "It's to show you that, you know, I really care about you. No matter what. Whether you ever end up wanting to be with me or not."

Rae stared down at the box, trying to decide what to say. There were too many emotions rushing around inside her, anger and affection and sadness.

"Open it," Marcus said softly.

Slowly Rae raised the lid and saw a tennis bracelet cradled on the box's satin lining. The sunlight caught on the diamonds, turning them into white fire. *Diamonds*. What was she supposed to do?

Rae. The moment Anthony saw her, it was like his body had a flashback. He could feel her tongue brushing against his, warm and wet. He could feel her arms around his neck. Instantly he was moving toward her. It took three steps for his brain to register what she was holding in her hand. It was that bracelet, that freaking diamond bracelet, the one Salkow had bought for her.

Anthony forced his eyes away from Rae, and, yeah, there was Salkow standing next to her with a crazy grin on his face. Why wouldn't he look happy after handing Rae a present like that? Salkow had acted all worried about whether or not she'd like it—he'd even shown it to Anthony to see what Anthony thought. As if there was any question that any girl anywhere wouldn't get all ecstatic at the sight of it.

He turned away and started back up to the main doors. What in the hell had he been thinking kissing Rae when he knew for a fact Salkow was getting back together with her? She deserved a guy like that, a guy who could—

"Anthony, wait a minute." Anthony's heart shot up into his throat, and his stomach lurched up into the empty space in his chest. Rae'd come after him. He turned to face her—but saw Jackie Kane standing there. His organs slithered back into place.

"You're out of the hospital," he said. A total moron comment.

"My parents wanted me to stay home for a few days, but I wanted to come back right away. Less gossip time," Jackie explained. "If I'm here, no one can say I died from my aspirin OD or that I'm in a designer straitjacket somewhere."

Anthony nodded. *Is this girl—this quiet, all-buttoned-up girl—the real Jackie?* he wondered. She was nothing like the girl who'd been chugging vodka at McHugh's party last week. Absolutely nothing like the girl who'd shoved him against the wall and kissed him until he could hardly stay on his feet.

"I wanted you to know—" Jackie took a quick glance over her shoulder. "My parents and I have our first family counseling meeting on Wednesday. In a few weeks my brother, Phillip, is going to come to one of the meetings, too."

Good, Anthony thought. From what Jackie had told him, make that what he'd pried out of her, Phillip was a big part of the problem in her family. "Was it hard to get them to say they'd do it?" Anthony asked.

"The . . . my suicide attempt scared them more than I thought it would. When the doctor told them I'd said I wanted family counseling, they fell all over themselves getting out a credit card and signing us up." Jackie gave a small smile. "I think they decided counseling would be a lot less embarrassing than whatever I'd do next. And all the best people see therapists," she added, more than a little sarcasm creeping into her voice.

"If you ever want to talk about any of it, you know, with a nonprofessional, I'm around," Anthony said. He noticed one of the laces on his sneakers was loose, and he bent down to retie it.

"Thanks," Jackie said.

Anthony retied the lace of his other shoe, even though it wasn't loose, then shoved himself to his feet. "I should go hit my locker."

"Okay," Jackie said quickly. She smoothed a stray section of her blond hair into her ponytail. "But first let me apologize for—" She hesitated. "For what I did to you at the party. I was—"

"In a vodka haze," Anthony finished for her, wanting to get this conversation done with.

"Well, yeah," Jackie admitted. "I was doing every stupid thing I could think of, like you said in the hospital, to get my parents to notice me. God, you saw me shoplifting and driving drunk—" Jackie stopped abruptly. Her cheeks turned pink. "I didn't mean kissing you was like those things."

Anthony knew kissing him was definitely on the list of stupid crap she'd done, but he didn't call her on it.

"It's just not something I'd usually do," Jackie rushed on. "At least not so fast," she added, speaking so quickly, the words came out jumbled together.

Message received, Anthony thought. *I get that there's no chance in hell anything's going to happen between us.* The first bell rang. "I gotta go," Anthony said, for once actually happy classes were about to start. "See you." He hurried to the main doors.

"Bye," Jackie called after him. "And thanks again."

Anthony gave a little hand flip, not wanting to turn back and be forced to look at her, then he pushed his way through the doors and strode down the hall. He got smiles and "hi's" from a couple of girls— more than a couple. But that's because he was good on the football field. That's the only reason they'd let him into Sanderson Prep in the first place.

None of the smiles meant anything more than "that's the guy who won us the game." They weren't invitations or anything. *So is it finally through your thick head?* he asked himself. *Jackie made out with you because she wanted to be a bad girl. Rae kissed you because you saved her life.* It didn't mean anything. *Rae—make that Rae, Jackie, and every girl in this friggin' school—wants to end up with a guy like Salkow. A guy who belongs.*

Rae hurried out the back doors and immediately scanned the parking lot for Anthony's mom's Hyundai.

13

She knew he always dropped his mom off at work so he could have the car until it was time to pick her up.

Good, it's still there, she thought. *It should be.* She'd sprinted out here—well, the Rae version of sprinting, which wasn't all *that* fast—after the last bell. She couldn't go the rest of the day without seeing him.

Was he avoiding her? Was that why he hadn't shown up in the caf? *If he is, it's because of that bracelet. He saw Marcus give it to me. I know it. And he went inside before he could see me give it back.* God, who knew what was going on in Anthony's head right now?

Rae decided to stake out his car. It was the only way she'd be absolutely sure he wouldn't slip by her. She started across the lot and spotted Yana Savari's bright yellow VW Bug. Perfect. She and Yana could keep watch for Anthony together while Rae told Yana about the bracelet and how Anthony'd stayed out of sight all day. Yana'd help her analyze the sitch. It was part of best-friend duty.

Before Rae could reach the car, Yana climbed out. One look at Yana's face and all thoughts of Anthony slid out of Rae's head. She rushed over to her friend. "What's wrong?" she exclaimed. "Did the guys from the motel come after you again? Did—"

"You know exactly what's wrong," Yana snapped. "Don't pretend you don't." Her blue eyes were bright with anger, and her face was flushed.

"What?" Rae cried.

"What?" Yana repeated, her lips curling into a sneer. "I can't believe you're asking me what. Are you going to try and pretend that you didn't know what I told you in the motel was a secret?"

"What?" Rae hadn't meant to say the word again, but she had no idea what Yana was talking about. "Of course I knew," she added quickly.

"You knew, but it didn't mean a thing to you. You had to be Little Miss Do-good and try to fix things. Just like you did when you went looking for Anthony's dad. Didn't that smack any sense into your head? You don't know anything about his life. And you absolutely don't know anything about mine," Yana spat out.

Rae forced herself to meet Yana's gaze, even though the fury radiating out of her light blue eyes was so powerful that Rae could almost feel her skin singeing. "Back up, okay? Just tell me—"

Yana shook her head, her bleached blond hair flying around her face. "Oh, I get it. You're going to pretend that you don't know anything about the letter." She moved closer, going almost nose to nose with Rae. "Did you think because you didn't sign it, I'd be too stupid to figure out who it was from? I only told one person about my seventh birthday and the ballet—you."

Rae stayed exactly where she was, fighting the urge to back away. "I still don't know what you're talking about," she said, forcing herself to speak the words softly and calmly. "What letter?"

"The letter to my dad. The one that told him how much his—what was the word you used?—oh, yeah, *indifference,* you said how much his *indifference* had hurt me. Then you told the whole ballet story. Not that I wouldn't have figured out it was you who sent it, anyway. It was so you, Rae."

Yana started to turn away. Rae reached out and caught her arm. "I didn't do it. You have to believe me. We thought we might be being monitored in the motel, remember?"

"Oh, right. And one of the men who kidnapped us felt so sorry for me that he decided to write a letter to my father." Yana jerked her arm free. "Just stay out of my life from now on."

"You don't—"

"Get away from me," Yana yelled. "Now!"

Rae felt tears sting her eyes, and she was suddenly aware that she and Yana were drawing a crowd. "Fine," Rae answered. Clearly it wouldn't help to talk to Yana right now. If it would, Rae wouldn't care how many people were watching. But it was pointless.

She turned and walked into the school building, then headed for the closest bathroom. Once inside she locked herself in a stall. The moment the metal bar slid into place, the tears started streaking down her face, hot against her skin. Rae pressed the heels of her hands against her mouth, pushing her lips hard against her teeth. She couldn't keep herself from crying, but she wasn't going to let anyone else hear her.

Yana was her best friend. How could she believe Rae would lie to her face? Rae yanked a handful of toilet paper squares out of the metal dispenser, then wiped her eyes viciously.

Enough, she thought. *Crying isn't going to fix things with Yana. I need to prove to her that I didn't send the letter. And that means showing her exactly who did.*

The only ones it could be were the men who had held her and Yana in the motel. She'd thought they might be listening to her and Yana, even though they'd been left alone in the room. Now she'd just have to prove it.

Rae threw the soggy toilet paper into the toilet and flushed. They—the men—had to have sent the letter to Yana as a way to get to Rae. Had they figured out how Yana would react? Had they been trying to make Yana think Rae had betrayed her?

It made sense in a twisted way, Rae thought. They knew Yana had gone to the motel to help Rae. So they'd torn Yana away from her. *They want me alone. That's what it is,* she decided. *They want me helpless.*

Well, that's not going to happen.